THE DAY I KILLED GOD

A NOVEL

NICK TOTEM

THE DAY I KILLED GOD
Copyright © 2020 Nick Totem

Lucen Geist Literary Press, LLC

This is a work of fiction. Names, characters, businesses, places, events, locales, and incidents are either the products of the author's imagination or used in a fictitious manner. Any resemblance to actual persons, living or dead, or actual events is purely coincidental.

paperback ISBN: 978-1-943564-08-8
ebook ISBN: 978-1-943564-09-5

Cover and interior design by Domini Dragoone
Cover images © Gyro/iStock and © Frances Coch/iStock

REALITY IS ONLY AS REAL

AS YOUR ABILITY TO PERCEIVE IT.

The dead girl smiled at me.

I had found her at the far end of a field abutting a grove of eucalypti, before the land turned up into a rocky hill. The killer had chosen the place because it was far enough from the road, but he couldn't go any farther. He had stood there, trying to think with his psychotic mind whether he should carry her body over the rocky hill. He had remained in one place too long and had left the deep impression of his shoes on the ground. At last, he dug a hole. And the soil had yielded to the shovel. But a foot down, the eucalypti's roots had stopped him, and the hole had been patchy at best. Then he had stuffed her body in and covered it with dirt.

From the moment I had paced around her room, picking up her personal things, her diary with a pink cover in which she had written "I love you Dustin" the night before she disappeared; her jeans and T-shirts with the faces of her favorite pop stars; her Harry Potter books, I developed a sense, like a hound dog, not a sense of smell but visual disturbance emanating from her presence. And I saw it strongly when I ran my hands over her pillows. Then, it was as if a part of the sky had turned dark, and toward that direction I would find her. I had rushed out the doors past her crying mother and drove fast toward the east, leaving Los Angeles behind. After two hours, I drove into the back country over gravel roads. I had to double back several times, and there I saw it, where the air was almost black at the foot of the hill, among the eucalypti—the place where he had dropped her corpse.

"Are you sure this time?" Ed Callow said to me as soon as he got there. He had always been the first to come when I called in a case. Ed was the LAPD homicide detective who had been my point man ever since I started doing these cases five years ago. He had a large Roman nose, eyes that always squinted, brown hair cropped short, and a slouching figure with powerful arms.

"She's there." I pointed to the mound of dirt under which her body lay.

"You didn't contaminate it, did you?"

"No."

"Anything else you care to tell me?"

"Nothing yet."

Ed shook his head. After five years working together, he still didn't feel comfortable with my sixth sense. "You give me the creeps. Remind me. You knew where to find her, how?"

"I just do." I shrugged. He wasn't really asking.

"They don't call you The Psychic for nothing."

I shrugged again. Psychic wasn't the word for what I did, but I couldn't share that with Ed. Then the rest of the police and forensics team came and cordoned off the area. They filmed the entire scene, must have taken a thousand photos, collected samples, and made impressions of all the footprints.

Afterwards, we were allowed to approach the site as they dug her out. She had been dead for about three weeks, so she had gone through the stages—rigor mortis, bloating with gas, and finally having her teeth, nails, and hair fall out. She was beginning to liquefy, and so her face had decomposed beyond recognition. Strangely, a butterfly with iridescent wings descended from a eucalyptus and landed on her cheek, and then it took off, circled around me a couple of times, and flew off. When it landed on her cheek, I could see that she smiled at me. It was not a hallucination; I actually saw her cheek moving and forming a deep dimple.

And, in a flash, I had a vision of the killer carrying her limp body. The picture was pixelated and fuzzy, like a low-res image on a computer screen, as if the air molecules held a memory of what had happened. He was tall, over six feet, bald, wearing square glasses, and had a beer belly. He had stood there, thinking, and he had stood too long. He had dug the hole and stuffed her body in. Then, the vision was gone; the fuzziness became clear as the air, and all I could see now was the field of weeds, sprinkled with poppy flowers. Between the earth, sky, and flowers, the place was beautiful enough to lie in forever.

Of course, I didn't tell anyone about how I saw her smile, or how I saw the sky turn dark, or how I saw the killer standing there thinking. They wouldn't believe me anyway. If Ed Callow were to press me, I would say that it was a psychic hunch as much as the science of deduction, that I was like a modern Sherlock Holmes, using my psychic powers together with the power of modern technology. But Ed had stopped pestering me years ago; he was always a practical man, taking what he could use and going on with his life in this life, never caring for whatever could be in the next.

The truth, however, was much more difficult for people to believe. In the end, the fabric of space would be torn apart; the earth itself would be in danger; and human existence would be questioned.

2

I was often called a psychic. I guessed that was the most commonly accepted description of what I could do. At the age of ten, I had survived a brain fever, and after that I had begun to have premonitions about things that would eventually come true. As I grew up, my senses got sharper. I could sense the presence of people, alive and dead. And I could see the haloes of the dead, always fuzzy and pixelated.

The world, however, had been changing—the spiritual world that I could feel in addition to the physical world itself. Two billionaires–Alan Munsch and Josh Baelz–had formed a space conglomerate to do experiments in space. Their space ship–the Needle–was now approaching its final coordinate near the sun; its mission was to detonate a gigaton hydrogen bomb next to the sun. The Needle's stated mission was to study gravity waves, but conspiracy theories abounded as to its real objective. The world, of course, protested but to no avail.

As for the spiritual world, I had begun to have a premonition of the end of the world three years ago. It was imperceptible at first, but slowly the world I had always seen in shadow had become more and more visible, at least to me. Lately, I had been seeing more strange things and having uncanny experiences that at once seemed more real than ever. In the past I would have a vague hunch, but now I was seeing the sky turn dark and zeroing in on a corpse fifty miles away. The new precision of my visions astonished even me. What's more, it wasn't just that I was seeing more of the world in the shadow; I feared that I was being pulled into that nether world—one I could sense but couldn't really understand. Fear swelled in my chest. While I had made a living knowing about that nether world, I wanted desperately to stay in this world. One day soon, I swore I would never do this again. But for as long as I stayed in this world, I would need money. There was no way around that fact.

A week later, the dead girl's smile, the fuzzy image of the killer, and the fear flickered on and off in my mind as I sat on my favorite bench, piecing together the second half of the case. I had found the body; now I had to find the killer. The girl's name was Gizelle Cumberland,

and she had lived in Torrance, which was near my old neighborhood. I had to go to her house again and walk the street, especially on this day, a special day in my business—the vernal equinox. After so many years of chasing the dead, I had gotten into the habit of noticing and keeping track of astrological facts because on these special days my senses were somehow keener, and because killers are often obsessed with astrology; I had to know their language. Tonight, I planned to walk the Cumberland's neighborhood and see what I could find.

For the time being, I sat back and looked out at the sprawling yard, at the afternoon sunlight filtering through the branches. Sparrow, Cockatoo, Nightingale were frocking among the trees as they were apt to do on a sunny afternoon; scattered among them were other permanent residents and newcomers, whom I didn't try to remember as they were likely to be gone soon. No, these weren't birds; they were names for the people, the residents of the McFadden Psychiatric Institute.

As for me, I had had a nervous breakdown three years ago. Things had become too unreal; the sky, the earth, the air, and the people had lost their substance. It had been a sensation with the force of an unbreakable conviction. One day, I stopped talking; I just couldn't get myself to talk to people. I sat around all day on a park bench, and they took me to an Emergency Room.

The shrink had drugged me up and transferred me to McFadden. Though I was free to come and go, I had been here ever since. I preferred it this way. I had a small room that opened directly onto the yard.

"Someone is here to see you," Rose said as she came up behind me. Rose Smith was one of the original nurses here; after her retirement, Rose had returned to McFadden after losing nearly everything in the financial crash, but she still had a keen mind and a love for her work. I didn't mind Rose's occasional snipes and snaps; we'd always gotten along just fine.

"One of those Wall Street shysters again? Tell them I'm not interested in picking stocks for them," I said. "Did you take money to let them see me? I'm not seeing them. How many times are you going to fool them?"

"Maybe if you gave me a stock tip, I wouldn't need to hustle them for money," she said.

"I don't do that. I don't use it to make money like that," I said. I had been afraid to misuse my ability; to abuse it would somehow condemn me. And so, I had vowed only to use my ability for good; that was what God would have wanted.

"Are you sure?" Rose stared at me.

I paused. Did she know something? She couldn't have. But it was true; I did use my ability to make money. Just before the Great Financial Crisis, I had sensed a darkness over the market. I had shorted the market and had made enough money to continue to stay here.

"Relax. It's a woman," Rose said.

"What does she want?"

"Don't you want another case? You haven't done anything the whole day but waste time," she snapped and turned away.

My face bent into a ready scowl, but I jerked back unconsciously when I saw a woman coming down the path. My jaw hung open, and I stared at her.

She was Margaret Dorothyne, later known as Margaret Spinoza. But for me, she would always be the beautiful Margo with soft skin, limber legs, and gently curving eyes that always looked to the stars.

"What are you doing here?" I asked as I rose.

"How are you, Daniel? How long has it been? Ten years?" She seemed to scrutinize the surroundings and smiled as if she was too polite to ask me why I was in an asylum. Her voice was deeper and more serious than I remembered. She wore a black dress that hugged her toned body and black heels, accentuating her pale skin, blond hair, and red lips. She looked fabulous, while my standard issued asylum pajamas made me ridiculous.

"Huh," I muttered. I still couldn't quite believe I was seeing her. I shook my head. I approached her and extended my hand, which she ignored. She wrapped her arms around me, giving me a hug, a deep embrace that recalled the last one she had given me ten years ago.

"I hope you've been well," she said.

"Yeah, yeah. I'm okay. Please have a seat." We sat down on the bench.

Then we just stared at each other for what seemed a long time. The last decade had deepened her features and shaded her façade with somberness. When at rest, her face matched my mental image of her, limpid and earnest, and still very beautiful. At last, she smiled an awkward sad smile.

"So, what . . . hmm?" I said.

She cut me off. "I've read about you. You've become really famous. How do you do it?"

"It was just one article in a tabloid magazine. Don't believe it."

"But I do. You know, I didn't believe you then. I always thought that you were just trying to comfort me. But now I do believe you. You really saw my father."

"Thanks," I said. Near the end of high school, her father had passed away suddenly. When I attended the funeral, I told her I saw father standing next to her. It was a fuzzy, pixelated image as well. "I remember. It was right after that, you got married."

She said nothing.

"So how is our man anyway?" I asked sincerely enough.

She rose and took a few steps.

"Do you remember what you used to call him?" she said, turning back to me.

"Yeah, I meant it as a term of endearment. How is he?"

"He's missing."

Elliot Spinoza, her husband, was my best friend in high school. We hadn't kept in touch since our graduation and their wedding shortly thereafter.

"Is that why you came?" I asked, somewhat disappointed; only now did I realize the subconscious hope that I could start something with her again.

"Yes. But I don't know. He's disappeared before . . . many times before."

"Yeah, that was why I called him the crazy. . ." I stopped and stirred uncomfortably. I had gotten a lot more politically correct over the last ten years; so, I tried to make up for it, "You know how he is. Strange, I mean, ahh, eccentric, given how smart he is. God, I read about all his accomplishments. The cover of Time magazine. One of the greatest living mathematicians. The youngest Fields Medal recipient ever. One of the most significant discoveries of the decade. It's understandable, right?"

As if she had hidden enough of her expression, she sat down again.

"He changed so completely after the accident. He hasn't done anything important since then," she said.

"What accident?"

"Three years ago, we were at the mountain house. It was late. I was sleeping, and he was up as usual working on his equations. He'd always liked working late at night. He said the sounds of the mountain winds gave him rhythm. He said he was onto a major discovery, finally solving one of those hundreds-of-years-old equations." Her voice wavered softly. "The most incredible shriek woke me up. I don't even remember jumping off the bed or rushing to the living room . . . But there I was. To this day, I just can't understand . . . I can't even believe. But I can't forget either. It's just stayed with me."

She seemed haunted. I decided not to press her about what she'd seen, not right then. Besides, something else was bothering me. "Three years ago, huh?" Elliot had called me around that time. "You know, he called me about three years ago. He asked if I could use my abilities to help him with an equation. I thought he was crazy. What did I know about math?"

"Oh, really?"

"He told me just to choose between two symbols. Alpha or Omega."

Her hands entwined, shaking visibly. I took them in mine and held them still. I had never seen Margo like this before. She had always been strong, opinionated, idealistic, and concerned only with the stars, which was why she chose Elliot over me. At least, I had told myself this often enough.

"Will you find him for me?" she said suddenly, squeezing my hand. Her eyes gleamed. I could see the blue irises dilate.

"How long has he been gone?"

"Five days."

"You said he's been gone before. How long did he disappear before?"

"Three days, five days."

"That means he'll come back," I said, relieved. "Don't worry so much. Have you reported to the police?"

"Yes, but they can't do anything. They said the same thing, that Elliot has a history of disappearing before, so they're not too concerned. They're looking for him. That's all they say. You have to find him." Still squeezing my hand, she brought it in front of her and shook it.

"Okay, Margo. I will," I said, but all my heart told me I should not get involved, for my own sake.

"Promise me, Daniel. That you won't stop until you find him. For me."

"Okay, I will," I answered instantly. I agreed, not because of her frantic pleading but because this was once Margo, the beauty queen who had reigned for four years in our high school, and more importantly, my once Margo. I would have to find some excuses later to back out. I was sure it would be okay, from what she had just said, Elliot would come back on his own. Nothing to worry about.

"Really promise me, Daniel. Not like the last time."

What she said stung me. After their wedding, they had asked me to promise to stay in touch and be their friend forever, and to be their big brother, but I hadn't kept my promise. I had vanished from their lives.

"I promise," I said.

At last she let go of my hand.

"Was there something different with Elliot this time?" I asked.

"No. Absolutely not."

"Then why are you so alarmed this time?"

"Something about the world has changed." She sounded like she was commanding me to agree with her more than simply telling me something.

I couldn't help staring into her eyes with astonishment. So, she felt it, too.

"What do you have to do to find him?" she added.

"Hmm. I'll need to examine some of his personal things. Like his clothes, his books, personal things."

"You mean to get a sense of him. Like a hound dog?" Her forehead wrinkled.

"I guess you could say that."

"Can you come tonight?"

"If I can. I'm planning on staking out a neighborhood tonight. I'm working on a murder case."

"Please come to the old house. Please do your best. I really need you to find him. Something is not right this time."

"You still live there?" Margo and Elliot lived in a grand old house near the beach. We used to call it the Mansion.

"Yes, we still live there. Mathematicians don't make that much money. And I do nothing but take care of him."

Abruptly, she stood and headed up the path as if she couldn't tolerate the air of the asylum for another moment. I followed her. There was one more thing I needed to know.

"Oh, Margo. You said that night at the mountain house. There was something you couldn't understand. You couldn't believe what?"

She turned to me and said, with a little shake of her head and staring eyes as if what she was about to say was quite obvious, "What I saw."

"What?"

"Nothing."

"What do you mean?"

"I mean literally nothing. Nothing was there. It was as if things, the air itself, had vanished."

3

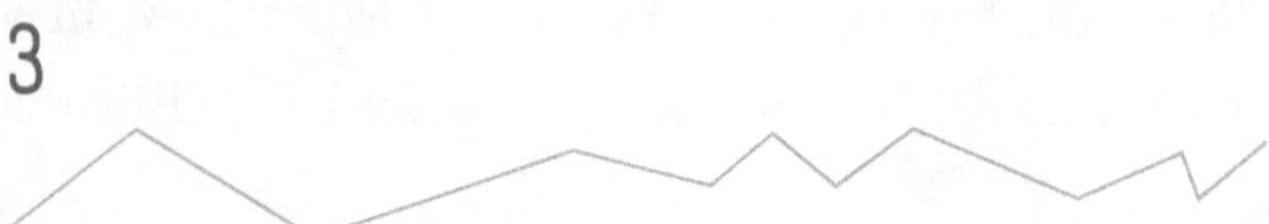

othing. She had seen nothing, which had scared her. It didn't make much sense, but I didn't press her anymore; it was obvious that she had become as eccentric as her genius husband.

Margo and Elliot had married right after high school, after her father's sudden death. Her father's family had come from old money and great wealth; as a widower, he doted on her. When he died, she inherited everything, and there was no one to stop her from marrying Elliot, who had become estranged from his father at the end of high school when she had just turned eighteen. I could still see them, a couple of kids with acne on their faces, gazing at each other as they took their vows. What did they know about love or marriage? Margo, who had her eyes to the sky, had only wanted a genius.

I had been in love with Margo in high school. Elliot and I, best friends since junior high, had met her during our sophomore year. That the most beautiful girl in school wanted to hang out with us perplexed us, but slowly we got used to it. I did my best to impress her, while Elliot was just Elliot, a math whizz. The three of us were inseparable until our senior year, when one day Margo announced that she and Elliot were going steady. I had always thought that she would choose me, but I hadn't been surprised. After all Elliot was a genius, not in the sense in which most people overuse that word nowadays, but the sense of Einstein, Newton, Gauss. Though his father had wanted him to be in high school so that he could develop normal social skills, Elliot had been far, far above any of us and just as eccentric. He had a special schedule to accommodate private instructions with the mathematicians and physicists at UCLA.

After high school, I, on the other hand, went to a community college and then a local college and barely graduated with a BS in psychology. I struggled with different jobs for a couple years until I decided to come to terms with myself and make use of my own natural ability. Then as suddenly, three years ago, I had had a nervous breakdown. I had decided to quit the world; I had wanted nothing more of the world or its people. I had decided to stay in the asylum voluntarily. Things had been going well enough until Margo came back into my life today. I sensed that things were about to change.

As the vernal equinox daylight lingered longer than usual and finally slipped into night, I couldn't get myself to go to Margo. I tried to suppress all my past feelings, the sweet yearning of a boy in love, and the ecstasy of the few times we had been together. All this thinking made me realize that I could still be in love with Margo. More devastating was the realization that loving Margo had perhaps caused me to be alone all these years, unable to form attachments to any other woman.

I decided to put off seeing Margo for a few days. Maybe Elliot would come home on his own. And the best way to forget about Margo was to find Gizelle Cumberland's killer. The Cumberland house was not far off the freeway in Torrance, and, incidentally, it was not far from the beach, either, where Margo lived. I started at one end of the street and strolled slowly along. Street-lights interspersed with large oak trees arching over the narrow street, giving it a secluded air. The houses were modest cottages, similar to the one I had grown up in. A gentle wind was coming from the beach and imparted to the air a refreshing briny scent. I had walked this street many times in the last month, days and nights, always with an empty head, hoping to hone into that the tug of energy, as in the past, when the killer happened to be near. A couple of days ago I had felt a fleeting surge of an omen, but I hadn't seen anyone resembling my vision—a tall, bald man with glasses and a beer belly. I walked to the end of the street and decided to turn left; I was determined to canvas this neighborhood until I found him. But my mind and senses were not as sharp as they should be; what Margo had said—about how the world has changed—kept intruding. At the end of the street, as I was about to cross the street and double back, a sensation came over me. A blanket of air, dense and suffocating, engulfed me from behind. My heart kicked up. My body seemed to freeze for a second before I could turn around. There, at the end of the street, I saw the shape of a man, tall and bulky, haloed against the street light. He seemed to stop as well and looked at me. Even with the length of the street between us, I knew it was he. I ran. He stood there for a moment and then took off. He made a turn, and by the time I reached the end of the street, I couldn't see him anymore. I was on the Cumberlands' street again, and it was empty. Unless he was incredibly fast, he must be hiding or had entered one of the houses. I scanned the street and gathered my breath. It must be him. Killers are known to revisit the crime scene, spurred on by an urge against which they are helpless, an urge which is as strong as that which drives them to kill in the first place. What's more, the killers seem to have a sixth sense and know when they are discovered.

Luckily, a car approached from behind me, illuminating the street as it went. I moved forward at a measured pace, honing onto that sensation, while a faint thought of being unprepared flickered through my mind. What if he had a gun? I had nothing with me. Even with his bare hands, he could kill me. Still, I must find him, counting on the fact that killers of little girls do that for a reason, that they are intrinsically cowards. The car sped off, and it was dark again. Was he hiding somewhere? I glanced back over my shoulder, but it was too late. He came at me fast from behind a car. I was on the ground; my head had hit the pavement, and an intense pain shot through my forehead. I crawled a couple feet. When I got up, I saw him running at the far end of the street.

I jumped up and staggered a few steps. I was about to run after him. At that exact moment, a screech tore through the sky. Through the trees, I could make out some changes in the sky; I was probably seeing things from the knock to my head. As if space itself had been torn, the shriek came from the direction of the beach, and only one thing went through my mind: Margo. I raced back to my car and sped toward the Mansion.

In Margo's wealthy beach neighborhood, the electricity had been knocked out as far as I could see, and car alarms were blaring along the street. I pulled into the driveway. The house stood imposingly against the night sky. It had three floors and occupied three lots. A line of tall trees surrounded the backyard, and the front door was unlocked.

"Margo!" I called out as I entered. The door was twelve feet tall, made of thick oak, and creaked as I pushed it. Light from my cellphone showed nothing out of the ordinary, and except for the painting of her grandfather hanging over the mantle, I didn't recognize the layout of the great living room with its high ceiling and modern furniture. Margo must have refurnished the place. I peeked into the library, opposite the dining room. From the back of the house, I heard static buzzes and snaps. An electric panel must have blown with the blackout. An anxiousness, which had been sloshing in my throat, abruptly swelled, and the pain in my head shot up; my senses were alerting me to something, I knew not what. Instinctively, I started to record with my phone as if it were now a crime scene. I swept the phone from one end of the library to the other; books of all sorts nearly filled the shelves along the wall and littered the floors. The desk, however, was neatly organized. I turned to the stairs.

An elegant staircase curved upstairs; I could almost see the beautiful and carefree Margo descending it. I headed up. Photos of Margo and Elliot lined the wall.

"Anyone home? Margo!" I shouted.

The static buzzes and snaps got louder. Directly ahead was the master bedroom. And I heard moaning behind the door. The door was jammed by something on the other side.

"Margo? Are you okay?" I shouted through the door.

The moaning remained the same, a sort of fearful crying and breathing that a child might make in the depths of a nightmare. I turned the doorknob and put my shoulder against it; I pushed hard. A piece of furniture moved on the other side of the door. I stepped back and then lunged, hard, forward. The bedroom door burst open, and I flew in. Instantly, my arms flapped backward vigorously to keep myself from falling. The phone flew out of my hand and landed on the ground below. Half of the bedroom was gone—roof, walls, half of the floor, half of the bed and the dresser. The empty space opened to the dark sky above and to the back-yard with the pool and the lounge chairs below. And the missing things hadn't fallen down into the back-yard below; they had vanished. It was as if a surgical blade had cut through a house made of paper, and the edges were infinitely straight and fine. A bluish light ran along the edges of the fissure sporadically, emitting static buzzes and snaps.

Suddenly, everything changed.

Every atom of my body vibrated, and I could see the energy from the blue light coursing through matter, pushing and rippling through space like a stone thrown into a pond. And I could grab it. Putting my hand to it, I felt it flow into me. My body seemed to inflate, my atoms rearranged, and finally they reconstituted. Only I was so much more energized. Though with a strong sense of déjà vu, I had seen it before, felt it before. And I was afraid.

Loud moaning disrupted my gaze. It came from Margo. She was lying on her side flat, on the floor, and her head jerked rhythmically, moaning each time. A web of fuzzy white threads zigzagged haphazardly, covering her head. I could see it and, yet through it, I could make out Margo's face clearly. The web was so fine that it was almost not real, but, try as I might, I could not disperse it. I pulled it one way, only to have it morph into another direction, as though it was a liquid and had a purpose, and that was to extinguish Margo.

"Margo!" I shouted, but she didn't move. I shook her. Her eyes were glazed open; the irises jerked sideways. I felt her pulse; she was alive and breathing. I picked her up; she was so light. I had to get her to a hospital. Though the lights were still out, I could see the way out as clear as day. In a few seconds more, I drove past the fire trucks and the ambulances screaming into the neighborhood.

4

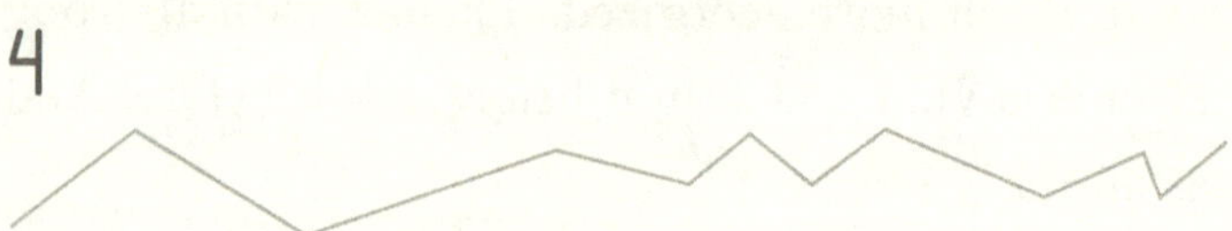

In the emergency room, I watched while they worked on Margo. I flashed the deputy badge Ed Callow had gotten for me and pronounced my name firmly, and they let me into the area where they tried to resuscitate her. I knew better than to interfere, I just stood there and looked on helplessly as a couple of doctors and nurses hooked Margo up to an IV, put monitors on her, and ran their stethoscope all over her chest. Even though I hadn't seen her for ten years, seeing the beautiful Margo like that really tore me up.

"Push the epi," a doctor said. "Open the IV line."

They stood back and waited.

One of the doctors appeared to be in charge, a serious man in his fifties. "Bring the crash cart," he said.

The strange sensation that had come over me continued. Perhaps it was the knock on the head, the incredible commotion that was occurring all around me, or the smell of antiseptic, but things seemed to flow and ebb, as if I could see the air move, or something beyond the air, something extra-dimensional. Yet my head was clear, and the pain in my forehead had gone; only the jagged ball of fear in my chest increased.

The doctor in charge approached me. "What happened?"

"Some kind of explosion. . . I found her."

"What kind of explosion, exactly? She doesn't have any external injuries, and probably no internal ones either. Her heart and lungs are fine. Her blood pressure is a bit low."

"It was dark. I couldn't see much. The electricity was out," I said. I wanted to ask him if he could see the web of fuzzy white threads around her head, but they couldn't be seeing it, otherwise, they would be trying to pull it off.

"It doesn't make any sense," he said and seemed to think.

An alarm suddenly chirped loudly, monotone, high-pitched.

"She flatlined!" someone screamed.

The doctor jumped in, barking orders, "Start chest compressions. . . Fire up the defibrillator. . . Get ready to intubate her."

Instantly, everything turned quiet in my head, and I found myself taking several steps back, looking with disbelief at Margo, the beautiful Margo, who had just walked into my life again this morning and who was now lifeless on the gurney. "No. No. Fight, Margo. Fight," I said repeatedly to myself.

There must have been five people working on Margo. They must have worked for twenty minutes, and then their actions appeared to slow. Abruptly, they stopped.

"Let's call it," the doctor pronounced.

Only then did it hit me; she had just died.

"No!" I yelled uncontrollably and lunged toward the gurney. I grabbed Margo's hand and the air itself shot into her; her body jerked. She sucked in a deep breath. The heart monitor started to beep.

"Oh, my God!" someone screamed.

They huddled around her again, pushing me out of the way. What had just happened?

"It's a miracle," someone said.

I looked at my own hand; it was unchanged. Now I was aware of the air pulsing like a vortex around me. I staggered back, hitting a portable X-ray machine. The X-ray technician was leaning against the machine and looked on with bored eyes, as if he had seen the same thing every day.

"Do you see that?" I said to him.

"Yeah. Sometimes the docs think they're dead, but no. I've heard cases where they wake up in the morgue."

"No. Do you see the air?" I turned and stared at him.

"What about it?"

"What about the web around her head?"

He glared at me. "Are you okay? Is she your wife?"

"No. No. Never mind." So, I was the only one who could see.

As the doctors busied themselves again, I prayed silently. "Please, God. Please save Margo. You gave me a special gift. And I've tried to do good with it. But now I don't know what's happening. Something is changing in me. If it is your will, give me a sign and I'll do whatever you want me to do. But please let Margo pull through."

After working on Margo for another half an hour as they had done before, probably doing the same useless things, they deemed her stable enough to be transferred to the ICU. I followed them and sat outside the room. Through the glass window, I checked on her now and then. She was intubated and hooked to a respirator. Bags of IV fluid were dripping medicines into her. The web of thread still covered her face. Poor Margo.

But what about me? Something had also happened to me. I could remember very clearly Margo's bedroom sliced off cleanly, but where did the missing parts go? Elliot Spinoza was probably conducting some sort of anti-matter experiments, and if that was the case, I could have been irradiated. The thought made me run to the bathroom. My reflection startled me. My black hair had turned white, almost shining with a bluish glow. In contrast, my face and brown eyes stood out as darker than they had been. After the initial shock, I checked every inch of my face; my nose was still in one piece, my jaw and facial bones still held all my teeth, and the whites of my eyes appeared unblemished. My forehead, where I had hit the ground, looked untouched; there was no sign of bruising.

I rushed out of the hospital, trembling with fear. I knew there was nothing more I could do for Margo. The early morning light streaked across the sky in separate bands of rays instead of the homogenous morning sky that I had known all my life. Then the sun followed the rays with an intense orange, lighting up the edges of puff clouds; the entire sky seemed tinged with a pseudo-reality. Maybe I was feeling groggy from a sleepless night. I had to go back to Margo's house; I had to see what had happened in daylight, and I needed to retrieve my cellphone with the recording from last night.

At last, I found myself on the street leading to Margo's house. My heart started to thrum violently when I saw that it was jammed with fire trucks, ambulances, police cars flashing lights, and unmarked government vehicles. Men wearing blue jackets emblazoned with yellow "FBI" were hurrying toward the house. Curious neighbors, some in pajamas, had gathered and were pointing here and there. At the intersection leading to the house, a cop manned a roadblock and was re-directing traffic. I turned left and right again on the adjacent street, hoping at least to see the back of the house. A black tarp at least forty feet tall had been erected all around the backyard, and another cop was there to discourage anyone from trying to get a peek inside. There was no way to retrieve my cellphone, so I kept going, heading to the asylum. I still had a couple of cellphones in the car I could use. Now I had no choice but to find Elliot Spinoza; he must know what had happened and whether I was in any danger.

Traffic on Wilshire Boulevard was inching along slowly by the time I got near the asylum. It was just past seven o'clock. The fumes of exhaust, the constant rumbling noise, and the honking seemed like any other workday, the normal functioning of the world, and I found it somehow comforting that I gazed at it for a while. I parked in the street away from the asylum. As soon as I got out of the car, I felt that something was not right. Two men, wearing black suits and earpieces, loitered at the street corner.

Immediately I turned around. Could they be looking for me? Did it have anything to do with last night's events? If they were indeed after me, they were searching for a guy with black hair, and so they might not recognize me. Cold terror washed over me, paralyzing me momentarily. My heart raced so fast that I felt it in my neck. I couldn't breathe. They must have found my phone and connected me to Margo's house. I decided to make a run for it. I headed straight to the car. I got in the car and started the engine. The moment I looked to my left to pull out, my heart dropped. I was staring right at the barrel of a gun.

5

The FBI headquarters was on Wilshire Boulevard, not very far from the asylum. They took me to the interrogation room in the basement. I was sitting at the metal table with my hands cupped to it, and it felt cold. Looking at my reflection in the one-way mirror, I saw how scared I was. Everything in the room seemed to have taken on the whiteness of the fluorescent lights, even time itself. I couldn't tell how much time had passed. They had searched me and taken all my belongings including my watch. They had drawn my blood, run a Geiger counter over me, and put me through a CT scanner; they must have concluded that I posed no hazards to them.

"Tell me everything about Elliot Spinoza," the interrogator commanded me.

"Why am I here?" I asked.

"You were at the scene of a crime."

"You mean Spinoza's house?"

"Yes. It's a crime scene."

"What crime?"

"Classified, but I can tell you that it's at the level of national security. Highest priority. Now, I ask you again. Tell me everything you know about the Spinozas," he said and narrowed his eyes.

So, I told him all the facts. Of course, I didn't tell them about my feelings for Margo, but any FBI agent with a little bit of acumen could have concluded as much.

"Where is Elliot Spinoza?" the agent sitting across from me said, after listening to my story. He had listened intently with his hands intertwined and his knuckles hard. Whenever he looked at me, his eyes seemed to glaze over and his mouth hung open a bit, making his jowls larger. His name was Jake Conme. From the slight tilt of the head that the other two younger agents showed him whenever they responded to him, I guessed that Conme must be pretty high up. Behind him, two other agents—muscular underneath their suits, with brawny square faces—stood at attention, as though they were trying to memorize all my words. As I would learn later, their names were Jack Royce and Jonas Ortega. Royce had a fiendish squint to his eyes. On the far side of the room, an older man leaned tiredly against the wall;

his head was partially bald, eyes red behind large square glasses, and his frame diminutive. He didn't look like the FBI type.

"I don't know," I said.

"Why did you run? Earlier today."

"I wasn't running. I just went to my car when you took me in," I said and tried my best to remain calm, while my gut was slipping to the floor. I had been in an interrogation before, with Ed Callow, but that did nothing to temper my fear. I was inside the FBI building, and I sensed that, whatever this was, it was big enough that they could hold me forever. And forever was not an exaggeration.

"Tell me what you saw last night."

"You have my phone," I said, pretending to sound clever enough to show them that I wasn't that afraid. "You must have seen the recording. That was what I saw."

"Hmm," Conme said. "What happened to your hair?"

"I don't know. You took my blood. You tell me."

"So, you don't know anything about Spinoza's work," the old man from the far side said as he came toward me. "I'm sorry to interrupt. I'm Professor Eigens. I need to know what you know about Spinoza's work."

Up close, I recognized Eigens from a TV interview; he was one of the brains behind the space ship Needle and its gigaton hydrogen bomb, which was set to explode at anytime now.

"Absolutely nothing." I shrugged. "How could I know anything? The only thing I knew about Spinoza's work was what I read in the magazines. Well, it depends on how easy they made it."

"Hah. I see," Eigens said.

"What happened to Margaret Spinoza?" Conme said.

"I don't know. I found her unresponsive and took her to the hospital. You probably know more than I do now."

Conme signaled to one of the agents behind him to un-cuff me.

"You have a knack of finding people. You're the psychic detective? Personally, I don't believe in such things but . . ." Conme said, nodding. "Spinoza has gone off the grid. We need you to find him. Beside whatever ways that you have, Spinoza knows you. That might be an advantage." He paused for a moment. "For national security and state secrets, foreign agents may be trying to get to him first. Or they might have already. Do you understand? You have to find him and find him fast. If you do, good things will happen to you. If not, then not. Understand?"

"I understand," I said. I didn't bother negotiating. I would have promised anything. I would have promised to turn over my own brother just to get out of there. Fear had made me that weak.

"Your blood work is good. The scan is normal. The doctor thinks you will be all right. . . Once you find

Spinoza, you're to stay on him until we can get him. We'll have an extraction team standing by."

"Okay."

"Anything else you want to ask."

"Yes. . . I need something from Spinoza," I said and caught myself using his last name. A pang pierced my stomach. Whatever Elliot had done, and I had no way of knowing until I found him, I felt as if I had just betrayed him.

Conme smiled as if he could read my mind. "What?"

"Something personal. I need to have a feel of him."

"Like a hound dog."

"Yeah, something like that."

They returned all my things, including my cellphone. Of course, the video of Margo's house had been deleted. The two agents who had stood quietly behind Conme took me to Margo's house. It was late in the afternoon when we emerged from the FBI headquarters. I was glad to see the sky again and to feel the air rushing at my face through the open window.

At the house, the guy in charge told us that, as a precaution, we couldn't go upstairs without hazmat suits, though they hadn't detected any radiation, or any chemical or biological toxins.

We went in, following a couple of men in hazmat suits, who went upstairs. They must have combed through every inch of that house, and they were carting things out. The chirps from Geiger counters came from upstairs.

The air had a rhythmic swirl in the library, and I went in there. One agent followed me, while the other one stood outside. He stood by the door and observed me, chewing gum and smacking his lips loudly now and then. Things hadn't been moved. On the desk, Elliot's notebooks were stacked high. A small notebook with a brown leather lay at the edge of the desk. Squinting my eyes and shaking my head slowly, I went around the bookshelves and ran my hands over the books. Abruptly, I stopped at one shelf and removed a book with a golden spine and beautifully engraved lettering. I flipped the pages and then put it back. At another shelf, I did the same thing. Finally, I went back to the first book and pulled it out half an inch. "That's the one," I said and pointed to it.

The agent leered at me suspiciously. He took the book and inspected it closely. He flipped the pages and even tried to read it; it was Charles Babbage's complete work. Meanwhile, I backed away a few steps, and making sure that my eyes were there to meet the agent's whenever he looked up, I pocketed the small notebook with the brown leather cover in one quick motion.

"I don't know," the agent said at last. "I have to check with headquarters."

"I don't want to get you into trouble," I said. "Why don't we just get his socks or something like that."

Before he could answer, I left the library with the little notebook safely in my pocket. It was a trick of distraction and misdirection that I had learned in my line of work. In the laundry room, I grabbed a shirt from the basket and said, "This will do. I can really feel him now."

Once we were outside, I told Ortega "I will let you know if I find him."

"Yup."

"Can I have a piece of gum?" I said.

He gave me a piece, and, with Elliot's dirty shirt in my hand, I walked away.

"Do you need a ride?" he asked.

"No. I'm good."

"Make sure you report in as soon as you find something."

"Yes, sir."

I went to the corner and hailed an Uber.

6

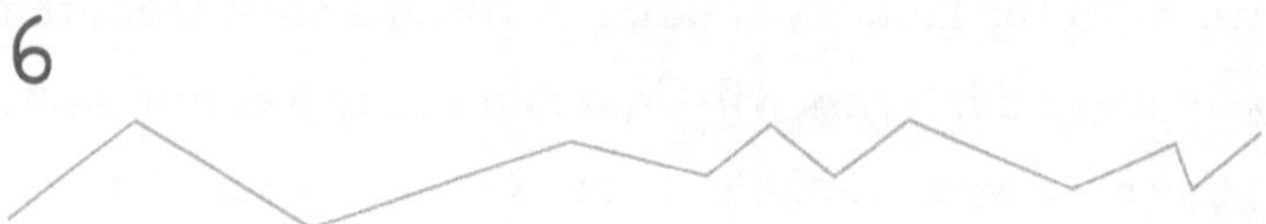

Five minutes later, a black Chevy Impala picked me up. I had entered the asylum's address into the Uber app, and the car was making good speed, passing through a shady part of town in Inglewood, when I told the driver to let me out. I wanted to go somewhere safe to look through the notebook; the asylum was probably being watched. Before I got out of the car, I spread the chewed gum over the camera portal and the microphone of my cell phone. And I left Elliot's dirty shirt in the Impala.

The summer sky had just tipped into darkness. I headed to a bar. The red neon sign above the entrance flashed: Sugar Bar. Motorcycles lined up in front. Even at twenty feet away, my nose could already detect a rancid smell of stale beer, sweat, and vomitus. Through the creaky wooden door, I was not disappointed. Weak lightbulbs barely illuminated the customers, mostly men and nearly a dozen, which was surprising, considering that time of the early evening. They occupied a couple of tables and a booth, and the chitchat stopped the moment I walked in. It seemed to be a neighborhood bar. The bartender was in his late forties and muscular, and even in the dim light, a "Semper Fi" tattoo figured prominently on his right arm. I took a seat at the bar, a couple of seats from another man, who appeared strangely fuzzy. As I waited for the bartender, I casually observed the people there one more time. From their clothes, manner, and physique, they were probably veterans, and probably in their late thirties or early forties. They shared a fatalistic, sarcastic gaze of the eyes. I could make out their features very clearly, except for the other man sitting at the bar, a couple of seats from me. A black fuzziness, similar to a flame, hung about his torso, and he sat like a block of stone with a beer bottle in front of him. His body did, in fact, remind me of a block of stone; his back was square and large, his arms bulged with muscles, and the fingers were like iron rods. The beer bottle was full.

Without saying a word, the bartender flicked his head in my direction.

"A Modelo please," I said.

The bartender popped a bottle and threw it down in front of me. "That'll be five bucks."

I put down a twenty-dollar bill. "Keep the change."

He nodded.

The other guy sitting the bar pivoted his head slowly to me and lifted his eyes; they were dull and blank, not a trace of life. Was the black flame around his torso really there, or was I just seeing it? But then I remembered Margo and the white web around her face.

"Were you in the service?" I asked the bartender, pretty sure that he would answer after the generous tip.

"Marine. Two tours in Iraq."

I sipped the beer. "What about him?" I looked over at the guy with the dead eyes.

"Cub? Navy Seal. Iraq, too. PTSD. His wife and son died in a car accident when he was over there. He's harmless though. You can hit him in the face, and he wouldn't do anything," he said and went about arranging liquor bottles.

I gulped down half the bottle and took out the notebook. I didn't know how long I had before the FBI guys showed up. They were tracking me but couldn't see or hear through my phone because of the chewing gum. Still, I kept the phone deep in my pants pocket. I could not get rid of it yet.

The notebook was full of very neat mathematical symbols, page after page. I couldn't understand any of it. Three quarters into the notebook, there was an odd thing, a blank page between a continuous equation, as if Elliot had purposely separated the two halves. On the blank page were the words: "Daniel, remember, beyond time," and a small photo of Margo was also lodged in there.

"Oh, Elliot. What happened to you," I said to myself. Suddenly, I was saddened by just looking at the hand-written symbols and words. All those tutoring sessions when Elliot had sat explaining algebra to me, those sleepovers when I had lain on the floor of his bedroom, looking at his star-filled ceiling, came to me. He had been a true friend. No. More than that, he had been my only brother, and now I was prepared to betray him. Elliot must have bet that I would find his message. He must need me somehow. But what did it mean? Was it a code for something?

Suddenly the door to the bar swung open, and I shut the notebook. A man wearing an army jacket with a bunch of medals pinned to it came in and started to salute the others. His reddish hair was combed slickly, and his face was wizened and tough. A lopsided overbite gave his upper lip a crooked twist when he laughed. He scanned the bar, and my white hair and dark blue suit must have caught his eyes. He headed straight to me as though he were the boss of the place.

"Harry, give me the usual," he said, standing between me and Cub. He leered at me and then slapped Cub on the back. "How the hell are you, Cub?"

Cub shook his head with slight jerking motions but said nothing.

"Winston, leave him alone. Do you have to torture him every day?" Harry said and put a bourbon on the counter.

"Put it on my tab," Winston said. He picked up Cub's bottle of beer, which had not been touched, and downed it in one gulp.

Cub seemed to awaken for an instant, and he turned to Winston and grimaced, but just as quickly he turned back to stare at the empty bottle.

"That's a good boy, Cub," Winston said and patted Cub on the head, which had short curly brown hair.

He was gunning for me next; I saw the usual bullying tactic, showing his dominance with someone he had already beaten down and then coming for the newbie.

Right on cue, he turned to me, "Who is your new friend, Cub?"

"He is a paying customer, Winston," Harry said.

"So am I," Winston said.

Behind me, two men stood up, sending their chairs screeching back, and came up to me.

Winston snatched the notebook from me. "What we got here?"

I jumped up and reached for the notebook, but one of the men behind me put himself between me and Winston.

Winston turned the pages and brought it close to his eyes. "Math? You one of those computer geeks?" he said and slowly sipped the bourbon. He walked leisurely to a table.

"Give it back," I hollered.

"How about you buy me a drink?" Winston waved the book in the air.

My anger surged into my left fist. The air pulsated around my fist, and I lunged forward, but the man in front of me stepped aside and in a quick motion pushed me from behind. I flew forward; my fist scraped by Cub's back, and I fell to the ground. I scrambled up; my hand, the one that had scraped Cub's back, felt sticky. A black mass, like a flame, was surrounding it. It had swiped it from Cub. I shook my hand vigorously, and the black flame just moved around with it. I tried to throw it out like a baseball, but it just shot out like a flare of gas and came back to my hand.

"What are you doing, geek?" Winston said. He must not be seeing the black flame.

In a flash, the man who had shoved me was next to me, and instantly I felt a punch to my gut. It hurt badly. I staggered back a couple of steps, still trying to shake the flame on my hand. He grabbed my shirt, raised his fist, and brought it down to my face. The fist stopped in midair. Cub's iron fingers had stopped it, and his eyes gleamed with a fierce, animal luster. In one swift motion,

Cub shoved the man back and punched him in the chest; the man fell backward and crashed over the table; and bottles and glasses scattered across the floor.

"What the fuck, Cub?" someone yelled.

Then came pandemonium.

They fell on Cub. Four of them surrounded Cub and threw punches and kicks. Though he had a physique of a rock, Cub was amazingly fast, and the screaming began. He ducked, caught an arm under his own, and lifted his shoulder; a crack was heard, followed by a scream. One man jumped on him, only to be flipped over a table. Another four took their turn. One went at Cub with a bottle, smashing it over Cub's elbow as he shielded himself. Cub jabbed him in the throat and the man backed away, gasping for air. From behind, a man put a choke-hold on him, but Cub pried the man's fingers out, bent them backward, and kicked the man in the groin. Another ran into Cub, only to be picked up and tossed up-side-down across the room. Now the rest of them stood back, shuffled around as though they were looking for an opening. But it was Cub's turn; he came at one with half a dozen punches to the nose. The man collapsed, unconscious, to the floor, and blood gushed from his nose. Then he moved to the next one.

Winston had been backing towards the door the whole time, shouting orders at the others. And he still had my notebook. The black flame was still on my left hand, but I couldn't wait anymore. I went for Winston. I took hold of the notebook and pulled; he pulled back. His other hand went right for my throat and squeezed. I couldn't breathe. My left hand with the black flame grappled helpless around his face. My left hand pushed hard against his face. Suddenly the black flame leapt to his face. And he screamed and fell back. Part of the black flame now encircled his head. His mouth gaped open, and his eyes glazed over like dead eyes. His body jerked violently and then twitched.

I bolted through the front door with the notebook and ran. Crashing noises came from the inside the bar as though Cub was taking down the joint.

Outside, the sky was dark, the traffic lights lit up the pavement, and I saw things so differently; I knew this because I was changing, not the world. Everywhere I could see something I could only describe as energy, flowing through the air, and things—cars, building, pavements, streetlights, and even the street itself— were warped with streams of energy coming and going and rippling like the surface of a pond. The energy was translucent for the most part, but sometimes they were the bluest of blues, the brightest of yellows, and glow- ing red flowing like the plasma from the earth's crust. It was beautiful.

I marveled at this new world. As I walked away, I had to dodge the streams of energy. I was very fearful at first, not knowing what it would do to me. But when one yellow stream came from behind and passed by my body without causing the slightest effect, I started to wave my hands at them. What was happening to me? Why was I seeing these things? Though I could see the streams of energy as if they were a distortion of the air molecules, refracting light through them, they flowed right through my fingers.

As I stood there with my hand dipped in a stream of energy, a black Suburban jumped the curb and screeched to a halt right in front of me. The shock made my heart jump, and my hand seemed to open up minuscule pores, so that the energy entered my hand. I felt my arm swelling and my body lifted. Two big men in black jumped out and rushed at me. They caught me by the arms and threw me inside the Suburban. The men got in the back seats and held me between them. The driver, also dressed in a black suit, leered at me and began to back out. Just then there was a loud pop, and the passenger window shattered. The driver's head hung limply, and his temple was bleeding. It had occurred amazingly fast, but I could see it; it was a rock thrown straight through the window.

"Get out. Get out!" one of the two men next to me shouted.

They probably thought it was gunfire. And the moment we got out, Cub was running at one of the men and slammed him against the car. The man chopped Cub hard on the neck, pushed him down, and hit him. Cub hit back once, but the other man, already behind Cub, gave two hard punches into his right kidney and grabbed his arms and put them into a lock. The man in front of Cub struck him across the face, and Cub's head swung hard. More blows to the face dazed him. After fighting the dozen in the bar, Cub was done for. I had to do something. I charged at them, trying to break them apart to give Cub a chance. When my hand touched Cub, the energy that my hand had absorbed shot into him. Cub woke right up and growled. He jumped up and, in the same motion, he shook off the man behind him, sending him flying back. He punched the man in front of him across the face, and the man slumped down to the ground unconscious. Instantly, he turned around, took three steps, and kicked the man on the ground in the stomach, which made him curl over.

"Stop!" I screamed at Cub, holding him back. "That's enough."

I was surprised when Cub stopped right away and turned to look at me. I bent down to the man on the ground and said, "Who are you? What do you want with me?"

Foam was coming out of his mouth as he struggled to breathe. I had never seen them before, and I had a hunch that they weren't from the FBI. Maybe they were foreign agents, as Conme had warned me. Then, I realized I too was breathing hard, and my heart was beating too fast. I got up. I had to get away. The FBI probably knew that I had plugged up my cellphone and was wondering about my location, what I was doing there, and they must be on the way.

After half a block of brisk walking, I felt someone behind me. I glanced back and Cub was a few feet away.

"Why are you following me?" I shouted at him, ready to run if he were to go after me.

His eyes avoided mine as if he was a kid. He stood very still. On the street, the traffic roared by, but on the sidewalk, we were alone.

"Well, what do you want?" I said loudly.

"Let me follow you," Cub said softly.

I must not have heard him correctly. "What do you mean?"

"Let me serve you." It was weird hearing such a soft voice coming from such a tough face—the scars over his left cheek, the square jaw, the saddle nose, and the fierce eyes.

"What?"

"I am reborn."

"Congratulations, but you can't follow me. Don't you have a job to go to? A family. . ." Then what Harry the bartender had said about Cub's wife and son came to me, and the black flame still surrounded my left hand, the flame I had taken from Cub. Perhaps he was reborn. Suddenly, I remembered the white web around Margo's face; I could pull it off her, too. I said, "Well, you can't follow me. I've got to go." I turned and started walking. I had to get to the hospital.

"You saved me," he called out.

"You saved me, too. We're even."

He kept up with me. "You performed a miracle," he said.

"Don't be ridiculous. I'm no Messiah."

"You're a prophet."

"No, not that either."

I was far enough from the bar that I called for an Uber, and so I had to stand at one spot to wait. The Uber app said the car would be there in five minutes.

"Every day I sat in that bar. I had no will. They insulted me. They bullied me. But I had no will. No anger. Only a lot of sadness. A blackness around my heart." Surprised by what he said, as if he had felt the black flame around his heart, I turned to look at him. His voice was rough, low, and sincere. He went on, "I was waiting to die. Everyday. Until you touched me."

"I didn't touch you," I said dismissively while looking

out for the Uber. "My hand just happened to scrape by your body. I was trying to hit that guy."

When I turned back to Cub, I couldn't help but jump back. Cub was on his knee, his head bent.

"What are you doing? Get up. People might think you're proposing," I hollered against the roar of traffic. And sure enough, some cars honked as though they were cheering us on. Someone even rolled down the window and screamed "Congratulations!" And there were others, who yelled at us to get a room.

But Cub wouldn't budge. He said, "My life is yours, Master."

7

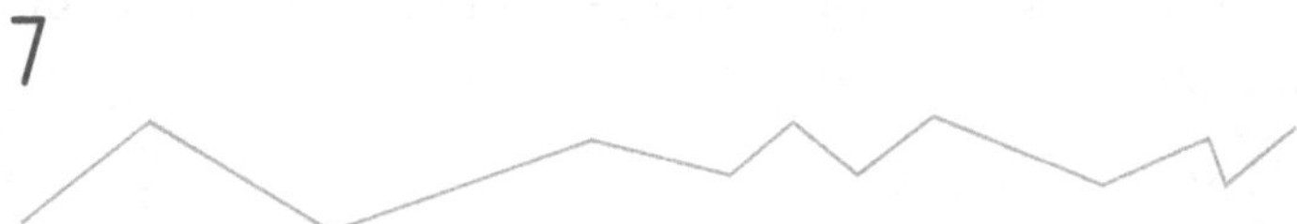

A Chevy Volt picked us up. Oddly, I felt no awkward-ness, sitting next to Cub. Now in a brighter light, I saw that Cub's cheek was bruised and the corner of his mouth was slightly swollen. He didn't say much more than to introduce himself. His name was Peter Brone; Cub was his nick-name, but I was in no mood to pry the story from him of how he got it. Of course, I knew that Cub would never say anything on his own.

As for me, during the quiet moments as the car car-ried us to the hospital, I dwelled on what happened to me. Apparently, I was still changing. I could see the energy streams more vividly, and physical objects undulating and vibrating, but other people gave no signs that they could see any of it. The FBI hadn't found anything phys-ically wrong with me, which was why they let me go. If they knew that I could now see streams of energy and even channel them into me and then pass it on, I would never be free. These thoughts stoke up my anxiety; my hands trembled and sweated, and my heart stirred painfully. I turned to Cub.

I raised my left hand and asked him, "Cub, what do you see?"

"I see your hand."

I turned on the overhead light and said, "Nothing else?"

"No."

The car dropped us off at St. Mary Hospital. We went in, and Cub kept a few steps behind me. At the front desk, two security guards waved at us. When I told a guard I was there to see Margaret Spinoza, his face became grave.

"Let me check," he said. He picked up the phone and spoke very softly, almost whispering, as though he didn't want us to hear. But I could hear him; my senses had gotten keener.

"What's the problem? She is in the ICU," I said.

"I'm sorry, sir. You can't go up there," he said.

"Why not?"

"You just can't. I got orders."

I turned to the elevator and started walking. From behind the counter, both guards came out, but Cub intercepted them at once and faced them down. He raised his powerful arms and stood ready. The guards looked scared.

"C'mon, Cub," I said. We went into the elevator. The ICU was on the fifth floor, and I felt trouble was waiting for us, so I told Cub, "Cub, I want you to pretend you don't know me."

"No, Master. I will die for you."

"Just listen. I'm going to try to save my friend. There is trouble up there. Here, take these things and wait for me outside." I gave Cub my cellphone and the notebook. "Pretend you don't know me until I call for you."

"Let me protect you. . ."

"No time to explain." I stopped the elevator on the third floor and pushed him out. "Listen to Master," I said and felt ridiculous for saying it. But strangely Cub obeyed right away as if my acknowledgment of being his master had made his rebirth into another world complete.

On the fifth floor, they were waiting for me. The same two agents who had driven me to Margo's house were ready in attack postures; their hands were ready for the guns at their waist. When the elevator door opened, they went in to make sure that I was alone.

"You can't be here," Ortega said.

"I want to see Margo," I told him as I headed to the ICU room.

Royce came up from behind me, took me by the arm, and pinned me to the wall. "You can't be here. We have orders to transport her," he growled into my ear.

From the end of the hallway, several nurses peeked at us.

"Where?"

"That's confidential," he said.

He pressed hard, squeezing my face against the wall just as a stream of energy was coursing along the wall. I could see the dry wall bulging as though a worm was burrowing beneath the surface. I couldn't move; Royce pinned me there, and the stream entered my eyes. "Arr-rrgh!" I screamed. The electric buzz fizzled through my brain and shot down my neck, and with a quick jerk I pushed back. An incredible force pulsed out. Royce staggered and fell backward. Anger, like a fire, erupted in my gut; the black flame on my left hand billowed out. Ortega turned to me as Royce got up; they both faced me. From the ICU, the nurses were wheeling out the bed, the respirator, and the monitors. Margo appeared lifeless, intubated, and the web still hung around her face.

I took a deep breath and said, "Please. I can help her. Just let me have two minutes with her. That's it."

"Stay back. We don't want to hurt you," Ortega said.

"I can help her. Please. Just two minutes. She will wake right up," I said.

They kept their eyes on me. The nurses and the machines passed behind them into the elevator. Then they backed into the elevator, still keeping their eyes on me. I wanted to do something. I could save Margo; I could lift the web off her face. I looked at the black flame. I could snuff them; I could push this flame onto their faces. But they were the FBI; what would I do after that? I exhaled my anger. Through clenched teeth, I told them, "If anything happens to her, I'll make you suffer."

They snickered. Royce slapped Ortega on the back and laughed out loud.

I took another elevator down and ran out just as the ambulance went off. I watched as the siren died away.

Cub was sitting on a ledge with his legs dangling; I called him.

"Cub, give me the phone."

I squeezed the energy into my arm and threw hard. The cellphone flew and hit the side of the building, dropped, and smashed into several pieces on the pavement.

Then I took the notebook. Cub just stood there quietly as I flipped through it and opened to Elliot's message. "Daniel, remember, beyond time." What did it mean? I still had no idea, and I flipped back and forth through each page. In the end I kept going back to the two pages; the page before and the page after the message somehow seemed different to me. They were full of mathematical symbols, and though I didn't understand any of it, they glowed and beckoned me. Those two pages belonged together, somehow. I had to find Elliot if I were to make sense of any of it. Our lives, mine and Margo's, were at a precipice, and, in fact, the world seemed near its end. Elliot was our only hope. I scanned the horizon. A bluish light distorted the edge of the sky in the east; I would find him there.

"Cub, I have to go east. I have to find my friend. You've done enough. You don't have to go with me."

"I go wherever you go, Master."

"Stop calling me Master. My name is Daniel."

"Okay, Master Daniel."

I shook my head at him. I wondered if he had always been child-like like this, or only since his rebirth.

"Okay, I don't have a phone anymore. We have to catch a taxi," I said and headed to the front of the hospital where a few taxis were waiting. "We'll head to my place to get some clothes, and then your place. We need to pack for a few days. . . We'll also need hard cash. Even though the world might end, we still need hard cash."

8

The drive to the asylum took about twenty minutes. The taxi dropped us off, and I asked the driver to wait for us. Everything was quiet, except for two men, clothed in jeans and black T-shirts, loitering in the street. They seemed to be watching us.

Without being told, Cub guarded the door while I went inside. I gathered all the essentials—personal items, and some clothes. I was still wearing my dark blue suit, which by now was very dirty, and so I changed to another one, which was much more comfortable, and a white shirt. As I moved around my room, I saw things in a new light, things that had held my life in suspension— photos of my deceased parents, a clipping of the only tabloid article about me, and nothing much more. A sadness hung in the air, but, more than that, it was a sense of pseudo-reality mixed with déjà vu, the feeling that everything thus far had been make-believe.

I searched for hard cash, and all I found was two twenty-dollar bills. All my money was in the bank, waiting for the day when I would disappear for good. As if trying to escape, I rushed out of the room and almost bumped into the Cockatoo, otherwise known as Mike Abe. Mike had been a high-flying corporate lawyer; he had specialized in hostile takeovers of corporations and had been featured in various magazines. One day he had disappeared, later turned up on Skid Row, and had been transferred here. Like so many people here, he had been diagnosed with bipolar schizophrenia with auditory and visual hallucinations. He had been the first person here whom I had talked to.

"Mike. What are you doing out of your room?" I said.

"A door opened," he said, looking past me. His hair was ruffled and hung to his shoulder, but his eyes appeared strangely lucid.

"Go to sleep."

"The door opened to outside."

"Outside where?"

"Outside to the real world."

That startled me. "The real world? Tell me about it."

He clicked his tongue and pivoted his head. His face twitched, as a side effect of the antipsychotic medications he took. "This is not real. I see it sometimes."

After all these years, why was Cockatoo telling this now? Perhaps he could also see the world changing. I raised both hands and asked him, "What do you see?"

"A face looking at us from out there. They see us. Clack, clack," he said, shaking his head, and walked away.

"Sweet dream, Mike," I said and headed out.

"Wash your hand. It's dirty," he said.

I turned back, but he had turned the corner and disappeared. So he saw the black flame. I went outside, where Cub was waiting.

"C'mon, Cub," I said and, without thinking, I put my hand on his shoulder. I felt as though I had known Cub all my life, and that he had sat at the bar and waited for me all these years, just as he had said. "C'mon, my friend."

As we left, I checked the street, but the two men who were out there earlier had left.

The taxi took to us to Cub's house, which wasn't far from the bar. Discarded bicycle parts, plastic toys, and overgrown weeds crowded the front lawn. A swing hung from a tree, motionless. Inside was not much better. Clothes, paper plates, junk mail, and a plethora of other things were strewn about. A car engine sat on the kitchen table, dripping grease onto the kitchen floor. A stench came from the kitchen and the sink that was full of unwashed dishes.

"Cub, listen," I said in a serious voice. "Listen. . ."

He was heading into his bedroom, and he stopped and turned to me. "Sorry, my house is a mess."

"It's not about that. You don't have to come with me. You've helped me enough. You should stay here and rebuild your life." The bruises on his face had completely disappeared. "Hah," I uttered as I studied his face; I saw kindness there. I wondered how such a kind face could have been trained to kill.

"Let me go with you."

"No, you should stay home. Spruce up this place. When I am done, I'll visit you."

"I'll go where you go. I'll protect you, Master. Please let me go with you. . ."

He was pleading, but I wasn't listening to him anymore; I looked past him. In the bedroom, behind Cub, a bluish silhouette of a woman flickered; she was folding clothes, and a little boy, may be five years old, was clinging to her leg. Then they became fuzzy at the edges, like a digital image, and vanished. His eyes followed mine into the bedroom, which to him must have been complete darkness, and came back to mine, questioning.

"All right. Come with me. Thank you. I can use the help."

"How many days should I pack?" he said.

"Maybe a week."

I waited for him on the sofa, a little concerned that my dark blue suit would be dirtied. Ripples of energy popped out of the air and vanished. While I tried to ignore what I was seeing, it was exhausting, and I was afraid that I might have a brain tumor. But how could I explain scraping the black flame off Cub and giving him a surge of energy to fight, and Margo's house being sliced so cleanly, and the web around her face? The black flame now burned around my left hand like a deadly weapon. All my life, I had believed that God had given me a gift, and it was only when I came to terms with it that I became a detective, to help people. Without a doubt, this was also God's doing. Powerful emotions overcame me, and I fell to the floor, kneeling, and with my hands together I prayed. I asked God to give me strength, to help me save Margo and Elliot, and, even if God were to destroy me, not to make me mad first, as Prometheus had once prayed. With my eyes closed, I kneeled for a long time, feeling as if I was merging with the floor itself. An emotional catharsis ensued, and I started to cry. When I opened my eyes, I was surprised to see Cub kneeling a few feet from me. His eyes were closed as well, his hands together and face tensed. I felt then that I could trust him with my life.

I got up and touched him on the shoulder. I said, "Cub, we have to go."

"Yes, Master."

"Do you have a car?"

"Yes."

His car was a restored 1969 Mustang. His hobby was to restore antique cars, which he had hoped to turn into a business to support his family once his service was over. The car was red with a wide white stripe running through the middle—his prized possession. Everything in it was either an original or a close replica—the tan leather seats, the chrome steering wheel, the analog radio with a slot for cassette tapes.

"This is a beautiful car, Cub," I said as he drove it to the street.

"When I was on leave, I used to cruise the coast with my family."

It was odd that he had said that because I saw his wife and son standing in the yard, looking on, not exactly at us but in our general direction. I wanted to tell him, but I decided to keep it to myself. Were they ghosts, who still had some sort of after-life consciousness and were watching us, or were they just phantasmagoric halos left-over from their previous physical existences?

"Where to, Master?" he asked.

I wanted to see if I could get some information, so I directed Cub to Ed Callow's house.

Past midnight, the Mustang roared, and the engine reverberated along the empty streets. Cub handled the stick shift with expert ease. For me, however, it was as if the world never slept; the flows of energy, the halos of livings things that had once walked the earth, and sudden sparks streaking across the sky were disorienting. Occasionally, there would be a normal living person walking the sidewalk. Then, suddenly out of the air, an electric silhouette of a dinosaur appeared and just as quickly vanished, and I would crane my neck to take a good look.

Ed Callow had managed to live comfortably in the suburbs of Los Angeles on a detective's salary. His house was a beautiful Cape Cod that he shared with his wife and two children. A white Lexus SUV and a BMW were in the driveway. Cub pulled up next to the front lawn, which was manicured and well lit. Cub wanted to go with me, but I told him not to worry and that Ed Callow was a friend. I went to the front door, rang the bell, and called Ed loudly.

The front light turned off, and Ed Callow came right out and pulled me inside. He said nothing and led me into his office, which was filled with boxes and files and smelled of tobacco. Photos of his wife and kids peppered the walls. He sat me down and poured me a cognac and one for himself.

"I heard they brought you in," Ed said.

"Yeah, how did you hear?" I asked.

"Me and a couple of FBI guys, we go way back. They told me. So, what went down?"

"I don't know. I was at the Spinozas's house. . ." I told him what happened. After I finished, I gulped the cognac; somehow it didn't taste the same to me, more like bitter, pungent water.

"So, you're recruited to find Spinoza. Any idea where to find him?" he said. He sipped the cognac while he glanced askance at me.

"Somewhere in the east."

"When are you going?"

"Tonight. . . The reason I stopped by. . . Ed, do you know what's going on? Did your FBI friends say anything about Spinoza? It looked like he was conducting an experiment that blew up."

"Sorry, buddy. They couldn't say. It's all top secret."

"I ditched the FBI, my phone, my car. Everything. They've probably frozen my bank accounts by now."

"I see. How can I help?" he asked sincerely enough.

"I will check back with you now and then. Let me know anything at all. Especially about Margo. How she is. Her condition. She is probably being quarantined at FBI headquarters."

"Really? I'll see what I can do."

At the door, Ed Callow gave me a bear hug and slapped three hundred-dollar bills in my hand.

"No, I can manage," I told him, but he insisted. I said, "Thanks. You're a true friend."

He kept the front light off, and I made my way to the car. Cub looked relieved when he saw me.

Then we went to the Cumberland's house. Not wanting the FBI to know my whereabouts, I couldn't use my ATM to get any more money, and seeing the condition of Cub's house, I couldn't ask him. That left the Cumberlands; they still owed me some money for finding their daughter's body. I wished I could wait until morning, or, better yet until I found the killer to ask the Cumberlands for the rest of the money, but it couldn't be helped.

The Cumberland's house was a small cottage, well-kept but aged. The wooden shingles in the front were cracked, and the white paint had discolored and splintered throughout. It sat in the midst of a middle-class neighborhood, and the lights were still on when we pulled in. When I took the case, they had agreed to pay me ten thousand dollars to find the body and promised twenty thousand to find the killer. They still owed me five thousand, though as I got to know them, I was very hesitant about taking more money from them, especially after praying so heartily to God.

I knocked and the porch light turned on. Martha Cumberland greeted me.

"Oh, Daniel. What brings you here?" she said, trembling visibly. "Any news?"

"No news," I said right away to temper her expectations. "I'm sorry to disturb you so late at night. . ."

"Please come in," she said.

Cub and I went inside. The living room had pink wallpaper. Photos of Gizelle at all ages were everywhere. Little dolls crowded a bookshelf, which was next to a small piano. The smell of roast beef was still in the air. Both of us barely fit on the small sofa. And I was thinking hard about how to broach the subject of money.

"Harold, Daniel is here!" Martha called upstairs as though I were a personal friend. She turned to me, "He's an early sleeper. Unlike me. Sometimes I stay up until the wee hours. Let me get you something to drink."

The sound of Harold stumbling in the bedroom came through the ceiling.

"No, that won't be necessary. We can't stay too long," I said. I wanted to ask her before her husband came down, but I couldn't. I sat there and stared at Martha. She was in her early fifties, and her age was obvious by the crow's feet by her eyes, the lines across her forehead, and her jowls. Gizelle had been her miracle child, conceived unexpectedly after many years of failed in-vitro fertilizations.

"Oh," she uttered. "Then what you have to say must be very important for you to come at this hour. Please wait for Harold to come down first."

"Well, you know how we agreed that . . . hmm, once I found Gizelle. . ."

Martha gasped uncontrollably when I mentioned Gizelle. "Oh, Daniel. We're so grateful for what you did. You brought our girl back to us. We'll lay her to rest once the coroner releases her. We'll put her next to her grandmother so she can be looked after. Harold and I will also come to visit her every weekend," she said; her eyes seemed lost somewhere, perhaps already seeing her daughter's grave.

As she spoke, her image fuzzed just slightly, as if the molecules had moved and snapped back in place, as if she were not quite real, but her suffering was all too real, so that even I could feel it. My heart broke for her. Just then, heavy footsteps thudded down the stairs. Harold was tall and heavy and had genial face, still sleepy. Next to him, a bluish halo of Gizelle also descended the stairs and looked up at Harold and then vanished.

"Harold, come, come quick, and listen to what Daniel has to say. He has news about Gizelle," Martha said.

Harold flopped down next to her, and they both stared at me. Cub too turned to me.

"I'm sorry to come at this hour. It couldn't be helped. I have to tell you before I go," I said. They nodded. Their look struck me silent. "Well. . . I want to ask you. . ." Their eyes were so full of hope that I couldn't help but say, "I fought the killer. . ."

"Oh my God. When? How?" Martha said.

"Just last night. I was out walking the street here. I saw him. I ran after him and he knocked me down."

"Master, I will be there with you next time."

Martha leered at Cub. Harold said in a low voice, "How do you know it was the killer?"

"I saw him when I found your daughter."

"What? He was there?"

"Not in person. I saw a vision of him. And I saw him again last night and he ran."

"Son of a bitch. He lives around here then. What does he look like?" Harold said through clenched teeth.

Of course, I didn't want to give Harold any idea or any chance of becoming a vigilante. I said, "Don't worry. I will get him."

"I hope we catch him and let them fry him," Martha said.

"I know how you feel," I said.

She shook her head in disbelief, and I couldn't agree with her more. How would I know what it felt like to lose a daughter? She began to sniffle. Tears dropped down her cheeks. Harold put his arm around her and said, "At least, she's back with us, Mommy." She nodded and dried her eyes.

I heard sniffling and turned to Cub. He was crying too; he must know exactly what it felt like. And I was sorry that I brought him here to relive the pain.

"We'll have a service for her. I hope you'll come," she said.

"I will," I said. "I have to go away for a while now. I have another case, but once I'm back. I'll catch that killer. I'll make him suffer." Without waiting for a response, I got up and went to the door.

"We only want justice. That's all," Harold said. "Justice."

9

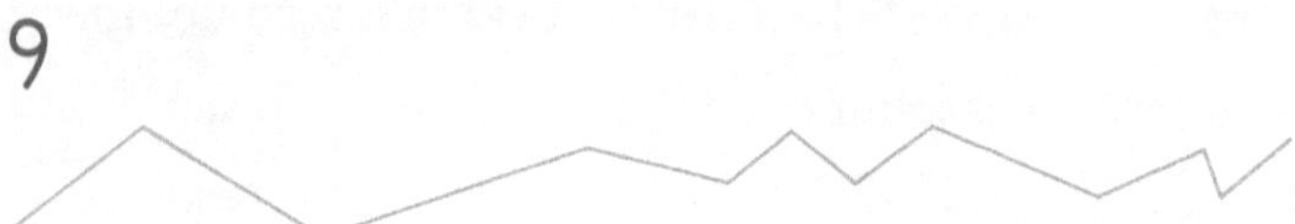

Human existence is an unfathomable injustice.

The thought hit me as we left the Cumberland's house. I told Cub to wait for me in the car; I had to be alone. Branches from tall Ficus trees arched over the sidewalks and shook in an errant breeze. Streetlights stood evenly along the street, throwing down cones of light. In the early hours, there was not much of this world; things of the nether world, the electric blue silhouettes of wandering ghosts from other times, things that only I could see, whisked through the atmosphere. A faint odor of pollen, sweet and nostalgic, came with the breeze and compounded my sadness.

Why were human beings created? Why are we given insatiable appetites that drive us on relentlessly, without a moment's rest? And rest could only come to the mental zealots like Mike Abe, who had all but renounced worldly existence. Why must the Cumberlands, who had been good all their lives, be made to suffer? What about Margo? What harm did she ever do to anyone? All she had ever done had been to look to the stars. Elliot Spinoza, my friend, and Cub? And what about the countless billions on the planet who suffered for food and water and shelter? What sustained them? Why them? That we were once animals means we would suffer forever; the needs of the body would always come before those of the mind.

A flow of energy passed near me, and I reached out for it, feeling it, and taking it inside me. And for a moment, I could feel all the suffering of the world. It was a profound sadness, an unfathomable injustice that we sentient beings must be made to suffer. Just then I didn't believe in God anymore. Even if he did exist, I knew I would never believe in him. Then inside me, something broke. I let out a long, deep-throated howl. No more. No more of business as usual, of being a sheep. Fuck everything. I would destroy them all. I wanted justice. Only justice would suffice. Justice. Justice.

Just then a gigantic column of energy, red-hot like a rocket, shot up to the sky from the earth, rippling the air. I watched it until it vanished into the edge of space, taking only a few seconds. Suddenly I saw that, deep in thought, I had wandered around the block without real-izing it. I scanned the street, and something dark in the distance pricked my nostril. I ran toward it. Even if dan-ger awaited me, I was ready for it. I was ready to be done with this life.

He was standing in the dark and peeking through the window. It was the killer, apparently stalking his next victim. As I saw him, he jumped from the shadow and ran. My sadness became anger, which burst through my legs. I got within a couple of feet of him and threw myself for-ward. I caught his legs as I fell. He, too, tumbled heavily; his glasses flew off. I crawled over his body, grasping and clawing, and started to punch him. I landed two punches, but he threw me off and got up. I jumped on his back and put a lock around his neck. He staggered a few steps and ran backward toward a tree. My back hit the tree, which knocked the air out of me. I fell. He stood over me and grabbed me by the collar. He stared at me. I saw his face change, contorting with anger. His fist struck me over the cheek. It felt numb.

"I got you. You bastard," I said, laughing.

He struck me again over the side of my left eye. And I saw double, the two fat, beady-eyed faces.

I laughed out loud again.

He growled and pulled out a switch blade. With a snap of his wrist, he unfurled the blade and brought it down. My left hand caught his wrist, stopping it. His growl got louder; he drew his arm toward his body so that the knife pointed straight at me as his body leaned in. I pushed on the energy into my left arm, stopping him. But the tip of the blade kept moving. It touched my jacket and went through it. I pushed hard against him and I saw the black flame on my left hand billowing out. That was my only hope. The tip of the blade poked through my belly skin and the pain cut deep. I screamed as I pushed the black flamed onto his chest. He gasped and coughed as though he couldn't breathe. A startled look came into his eyes, and he leaned toward me as though he knew he had to kill me first. The blade slid in. I clenched my teeth and expelled all I had into my left arm. The black flame shot out, but as it did so, the killer flew off me. The black flame blew into the air.

"Are you okay, Master?" Cub was next to me. Cub had thrown the killer off me.

I felt my abdomen; it was wet with blood. A few feet away, the killer got up, still holding the knife.

"Get him, Cub," I said.

Cub got up and, with slow, sure steps, approached the killer. As if the smell of blood had made him bold, the killer stood there waiting. He thrust the knife at Cub. Cub jumped back and then quickly moved forward and hit him in the face. The killer threw another jab. Again,

Cub jerked back. I knew Cub was testing him, to see all his moves. Cub moved tantalizingly close to the killer, inviting the knife. The killer lunged forward, and with a graceful move, Cub led him to a side and jabbed him hard just below the rib cage. Cub bounced on his feet, now toward the killer, then away from him. It was a deadly dance and a marvel to see. At last, at another thrust of the knife, Cub ducked sideways, caught the killer's wrist, and punched hard against his elbow. The knife flew to the ground with a clang. Then Cub darted toward the killer, hitting repeatedly him in the belly, which made him bend over. And a hard hit on the back of the neck felled the killer. He passed out on the ground. Cub turned over him, sat over him, and let loose his fists.

I was afraid Cub would kill him. I grabbed Cub's arm, and he stopped.

I stood over the killer to take a good look, and he was the vision I saw when I found Gizelle's body. As though he was ashamed of losing his control, Cub left me to pick up the knife. Kneeling down next to the killer, I slapped him.

"Wake up," I said.

The killer muttered a few sounds.

I slapped him hard across the face. He came to and tried to sit up, but Cub put his knee on the killer's chest and pinched him down. He put the knife right under the killer's chin.

"You killed Gizelle, didn't you?" I said.

He was fully conscious now. His beady eyes beat sideways.

"Let me go," he said and tried to wriggle from under Cub's knee.

Cub pushed the knife and the killer lifted his face. A thin line of blood drifted down his neck from where the knife stuck him.

"Don't try to move, or that knife will go straight into your mouth," I said. I held Cub's hand back so the killer could move his jaw to talk. "One last time. Did you kill Gizelle?"

"You got nothing on me. This won't hold up in court. You're crooked cops. You attacked me in the middle of the street."

I felt his pocket and took out his wallet. The driver's license read: David Mageet. It was a Michigan license.

"You're right," I said. "None of this will hold in court. But then again, we are not cops. Tonight is your lucky night." I held up my left hand and flicked the black flame. "Do you see this?"

I wondered if he could really see it because he seemed terrified.

"Don't hurt me. I'll tell you. Take me in," he said, trembling.

I channeled my strength into the flame and brought

it down to his heart. He squealed meekly. I pulled up the flame and said, "Confess to me. Here is your chance."

He looked into my eyes and said, "I didn't mean to. I only wanted to love her."

"How many more before her?"

"Six."

My heart sank. I said, "You will go away now. To a place where you can never hurt another little girl again."

I didn't know exactly what the black flame would do to him. I brought the flame to his face. My anger and sadness flared through my hand. The black flame engulfed his head. He twitched as if having a seizure, and then he spoke, as if to himself, gurgling sounds.

I got up and told Cub to let him go. The killer got up, took a few steps, and flopped down on the ground. His hands gesticulated and from his mouth came the same gurgling sounds.

"Let's go, Cub," I said and went to the car.

"What did you do, Master?" Cub asked.

"I don't really know. Maybe I put him away forever."

"Are you hurt?"

"Not so bad." The bleeding had stopped, and the wound was already healing. "Thanks for coming. And don't call me Master anymore. I'm your friend."

At the car, I changed my shirt, and we drove east into the desert.

In the morning, I would call Ed Callow and tell him about the killer. The next day when they raided his house, they would find locks of hair, clothing, and even photos of the six other victims. Unfortunately, because the killer was now in a catatonic state, he couldn't say anything about the whereabouts of the other victims' bodies.

10

From Los Angeles, we headed east and then north to Las Vegas. The horizon beckoned me that way; Elliot was in that direction. At nearly two in the morning, the road was empty and was imbued with a quiet peace. The constant rumble of the engine and the beams of the headlights pushed through something other than the darkness, moving through not empty space but a fluid medium, one which only I could see. The night sky was filled with ghosts, at times flickering with a greenish or bluish hue, outlines of all the living things that had once existed on earth. On occasion, a column of technicolor light shot straight to space and another descended from outer space and disappeared into the crust of the earth.

Even in this never-seen-before landscape, I was over-come with nostalgia. Margo, Elliot, and I had driven to

Las Vegas this way years before, in the last month of high school. Perhaps Margo had mentioned it as a joke, and Elliot and I pretended to go along facetiously. We would get drunk, stuff ourselves at the buffets, and gamble, we said. It must have been the abandonment of graduating from high school, and soon we were in Margo's BMW heading to Vegas, armed with fake IDs and her credit cards. The Flamingo Casino welcomed Margo's money and overlooked our fake IDs. We did as we said, getting drunk and stuffing ourselves. Margo and I fed Elliot oysters and vodka, which he had never had before, and which confined him to the bathroom for over an hour. When he emerged, vomit slime streaked his face and hair, but Margo didn't laugh at him as I did; she promptly wetted a towel and cleaned him. It was the first sign of true affection, which I didn't recognize then. We stayed in Vegas for only one night and drove home the next day, each of us a little changed; looking back, I could now see that by then Margo had already decided to be with Elliot.

Nostalgia never comes to you by itself; it always brings friends—sadness and regret. I should have stayed connected to my friends, who were now my only family in this world. After Margo's father died, she only had Elliot and me. It was a rare confluence of chance that Elliot's estrangement from his father, a hedge-fund analyst, and my parents' deaths made each of us the closest thing the others had. It was my failing, my pride and hurt, that had made me stay away from them.

"What happened to your family?" I asked Cub and immediately cringed. Perhaps nostalgia had made me reach out to Cub.

We were deep in the desert, more than halfway to Vegas. As usual, Cub sat like a rock and showed no sign of fatigue.

"They died," he replied as-matter-of-factly.

"I am so sorry. We don't have to talk about it."

"They died when I was in Iraq," he went on.

Wanting to know as much about him as possible, I nudged him a little bit. "The bartender said they were in a car accident."

"My wife shot my son and then killed herself."

"Oh my God, I'm so sorry."

"Depression. She struggled for years. When I was home, she seemed okay. But every time I left, she had a hard time. On the last tour I couldn't come home like I had promised. A Taliban leader was spotted in Helmand. Our team was dispatched for a surgical strike to take him out, dead or alive. It was a trap. We lost half of our team." He spoke with a monotone. "It took two days before they could extract us. And the first thing they told me when I got off the helicopter was to call home. . ."

"What do you mean?"

"Later on, when I was at a base in Germany, I deserted. I'd had enough. . . . They arrested me. A court-martial found me guilty with extenuating circumstances. I was dishonorably discharged with no prison time."

"Your son was about five years old," I said.

Cub turned to me. "Did you see him?"

"I did. At the house. And your wife, too. A beautiful woman."

Abruptly, he turned toward the road as tears dropped down his face.

"I'm sorry, Cub. I didn't mean to make you relive your pain."

"It's okay. You helped me. I don't know what you did, but I felt myself again when you touched me. Before that, I was filled with sadness, without hope. How did you do it?"

"The truth is, I don't know what I did," I said and looked at my left hand. The black flame flickered. Cub couldn't see it, but Mageet the killer of little girls could. "Why do you call me Master? I'm just a man like you."

"I felt the holiness in you. I felt it whenever you touched me."

He must be referring to the times when I passed the energy to him. That got me thinking about this nether world, in which there were rules, too. I could see the energy and capture it, but I couldn't harness it to be stronger, the way Cub could use it. I could see the dark energy and scrape it off Cub, which now stuck to my left hand as a black flame, and I could push it onto others. I had pushed it onto Mageet. Apparently, the black flame sickened anything that it touched, including the minds—Mageet's and before that, Cub's. And there must be others who could see the way I saw things; Mageet, the killer, saw the black flame. There were still too many questions, such as what had cut up Margo's house in half, what had deranged her mind, and why dead things were appearing in electric silhouettes.

"Holiness? I don't even believe in God anymore."

"Do you think the bomb will destroy the sun?" Cub asked abruptly, apparently attributing to me not just holiness but scientific knowledge.

"I wouldn't know, Cub. Though I doubt it."

Then the Mustang descended, and from afar the electric glow of Las Vegas brightened the night sky.

What about Elliot? Could he now see this nether world as well? More importantly, could he explain to me what was happening? And why did a premonition of our world ending weigh so heavily in my heart? I must find Elliot. Thinking of him, I reached into my jacket for the notebook. *It was gone.*

11

"Stop the car," I yelled at Cub. The car screeched to a stop. I jumped out and looked everywhere, under the seat, in the trunk, in my bag, but the notebook was gone. It must have fallen out of my pocket during the struggle with Mageet.

As I stood in the desert, under the stars, I closed my eyes. The light of a passing car brightened the night and then darkness quickly resumed. I concentrated to see if I could remember where I had dropped the notebook. Instead, I saw the equations, word for word, symbols for symbols. It was as if my mind had taken a photo of it. In my mind, I could turn the pages, back and forth. I could read Elliot's message, "Daniel, remember, beyond time," as though it was right in front of me.

"What did you lose?" Cub asked as he hustled about trying to help me despite not knowing what he was looking for.

"The notebook. But it's okay. Let's get to Vegas. You need to rest," I said. As for myself, I was neither tired nor sleepy, only anxious to find answers.

The glitz, the blinking neon lights, and the flashing of gigantic screens over Las Vegas Boulevard almost resembled the nether world. In fact, as we cruised down Las Vegas Boulevard, I saw everywhere visions of the past. Once the electric blue of a Native American dressed in leather and headband, armed with a tomahawk, raced across the street and went right through us, and I had to close my eyes. Electric-blue silhouettes of prostitutes, drunks, and lost souls from the past seemed to litter the very air, and sometimes they acted as if they were still living.

I told Cub to go to the Flamingo Hotel, where Margo, Elliot, and I had gone in high school. After a major renovation, the hotel now had a beautiful lobby decorated very tastefully with pink accents and was filled with the digital sounds of slot machines, the distant yells of the few remaining gamblers, and the low shushing noise of some unidentifiable happenings. The smell of cigarette smoke and air freshener mixed oddly in the air. A sleepy-eyed attendant checked us in. We had to use Cub's credit card to get a room; I felt horrible about it, about using whatever money Cub had. Though I made my misgivings about using his money obvious enough and promised to pay him back, he didn't seem to care; his deference to me seemed to only increase. He insisted on carrying my bag and did everything for me, including leading me to the room. When I passed a mirror and caught a reflection of my image, I was shocked once again by the whiteness of my hair. I hadn't yet gotten used to it. Other guests ogled us as though I were someone very important.

It was near six in the morning when we entered our room. I told Cub to get some sleep. I, on the other hand, was not tired, hungry, or thirsty. I decided to go to the lobby to clear my thoughts, and in truth I also wanted to try my skill at the gambling table. After all, we were desperate for money, and we would need a lot of it to find Elliot.

Before I had vowed to use my ability only for good, I had had success at the blackjack table; my premonition had brought winning of a couple thousand dollars. I had never been a big gambler, but then again, my ability had never been like it was now.

I sauntered through the largely deserted floor, the aisles lined by gaming tables; the dealers stood still as statues, eyeing me. I nodded and smiled at them. Then

Bugsy Siegel appeared and walked past me; his hair was sleekly combed, his suit impeccable, and his loafers shining; and he flashed a crooked smile at me as though he could see me, which startled me so that I had to stop and gaze after him. Was he a ghost haunting this place? After all, the Flamingo was his baby.

The only action was at the roulette table, so I headed there. If I were to try something, I wanted to have cover from other gamblers. There were two men and a woman placing bets, and a few more people stood behind them, apparently their spouses or partners, cheering them on. First, I watched the wheel and the ball to see if I could get a sense of where it was landing, the same way that I could see the dark halo over the horizon where I had found Gizelle's body. The wheel spun in the opposite direction of the ball, and the dealer could vary the speed of the ball. Ordinarily, it would be impossible to predict where the ball would land, and on previous occasions I had tried but could never predict where the ball would fall. Now I watched the wheel and the ball intently; they raced fast against each other, but as they slowed, I could mentally map ahead and see where the ball would fall. The first time, the ball fell into number 11, as I had predicted it would, and it must have been a lucky guess. The second time, I saw that it was heading to number 35, but it fell into the next slot, number 23. The third time, I predicted number 36, but it fell into number 13, also the adjacent slot. I did this a few more times until I determined that I could predict within three numbers where the ball would fall.

Then I was ready. I changed the three hundred dollars Ed Callow had given me, and I was careful to spread my bets around thinly at first. After a couple of spins, I tripled up on the three numbers that I saw the ball falling into. I won twice, and then I purposely lost three times, always losing small bets. I played twelve spins and won over two thousand dollars. The other gamblers were beginning to bet with me.

"You're on a roll, man," the woman next to me said. She was in her late sixties, somewhat chubby, and had blonde hair with black roots. She added, "Mind if I bet with you?"

"Go right ahead," I replied and purposely lost the next couple of spins.

Then, just when the dealer was about to wave his hand over the table to stop all bets, I quickly put down two hundred-dollar chips each over the three numbers. The ball fell right in the middle of the three numbers. People around screamed and gave me high fives. The dealer's face blanched, and he called the pit boss over before he paid me. I had enough money now, so I decided to quit, perhaps trying again at another casino. More importantly, my ability now would ensure that I could always make money, if I could keep it hidden.

"Can you cash me in?" I asked the dealer loudly as though speaking to everyone around, "I'd better quit when I'm ahead."

I gave the dealer a hundred-dollar chip. Walking past the blackjack table, I felt something tugging at me. I glanced in that direction and was startled by Bugsy Siegel, his ghost standing behind the dealer, staring straight at me. He flicked his chin beckoning me to the table as if he had something to tell me. I couldn't resist. Still keeping my eyes on him, I went to the table and put down my chips.

"Good morning," the dealer said and took a card from the shoe.

But I was still looking at Siegel, fuzzing statically, like electricity, and I couldn't believe it. He licked his lips and was about to say something. Was he real? Was it possible?

"Huh, hmm," the dealer said.

I put down a hundred-dollar chip while keeping my eyes on Siegel, trying to pull the words from his mouth.

The dealer opened the cards.

"Go up," Siegel's lips seemed to mime.

I leaned forward, squinting. Was the ghost of Bugsy Siegel talking to me?

"Sir," the dealer said and followed my eyes and peeked over his shoulder, and then, seeing nothing, he turned back to me with a puzzled look.

I had a six and a seven. The dealer had a three show-ing, and under his three was a seven. I wasn't supposed to draw, but I saw the next card in the shoe, actually see-ing through it. I had to look twice. It was a three. Could I really see through the card? I had to make sure. As soon as I tapped on the table, the dealer opened the card. It was just as I'd seen. The next card was a queen of spade, so I stopped. Either way, I was going to lose.

When I looked up, Siegel was gone. The dealer opened the card, which was a queen, and took my chips. Just then the dealer appeared to fuzz a little, pixelating like Bugsy Siegel, which made me think that I was playing with a ghost. I had an overwhelming sense that none of this was real, not the dealer, the table, the cards, or even I. I looked down at the chips. They weren't equivalent to money, to ten thousand dollars that I had known all my life, and they weren't any more real than the ghosts. I put them all on the table.

The dealer stared at me for a second and said, "You're playing it all?"

I nodded.

He counted the chips, which totaled nearly nine thousand, and looked over to the pit boss. The pit boss walked slowly to the table and adjusted his glasses to ogle the table and then me. He was an old man wearing an old, but nicely pressed suit, a white shirt, a blue tie, and a grim wizened face. He waved.

The dealer flipped the card. I had a seven of clubs and a four of diamond. The dealer's card was an eight of spades, and I could see that the dealer's other card underneath was a six of diamonds. I pulled the next card, an ace of diamonds, and then I stopped. The dealer had to ask me again. I waved my hand across the table.

"No more cards?" the dealer asked. I was sure that he couldn't believe what he was seeing.

"No," I told him.

The pit boss leaned in and stared at the cards. The dealer uncovered his card, which was as I had seen, a six. He pulled another card, which was a queen of hearts. Shaking his head, he turned to the pit boss and shrugged. Then he counted the chips and pushed them to me.

"Let it ride," I told him.

"The limit of the table is ten thousand," he said; his voice was steady and calm.

"Then raise the limit."

The pit boss went to make a phone call, and a moment later, he came back and removed the limit sign. Of course, the dealer didn't stand a chance. I saw the cards even before they were dealt and won the next two hands by holding a hand of nine and another of fifteen. There were now nearly seventy-two thousand dollars on the table. A few people had approached the table and were watching at a distance, talking among themselves.

"Sir," someone behind me said.

Two men wearing cheap black suits and earpieces, with buzz cuts and big, round faces, were staring at me. They couldn't be a more generic pairs of security guards.

"Yes, what do you want?" I said.

"You have to come with us," one of them said.

"Why? I'm on a roll. A guy can't win? He can lose but if he starts to win, no. Can't have that. No way."

"Please come with us," a guard said monotonously.

I turned to the dealer and pit boss and said, "Cash me out. You heard your boss."

It was the first time in my life that I held the ten-thousand dollar chips, and they felt fake, just like everything else. I followed the guards, heading to the elevator and wondering what story they would come up with to take my winnings. Truth be told, despite the world changing, I was still scared because I lived in this world. And technically, I did cheat, so I didn't care if they took the money.

They led me away from the table.

"Hey, I'm not going to go with you," I said. "I'm going back to my room."

"You have to come with us," the same guard repeated.

"I don't have to do anything." I stared down at my left hand and flicked it so that the black flame twirled.

"Please come with us. We're just doing our job."

"If you guys are trying to scare me and take the chips, it's not going to work. I didn't cheat. You guys can rewind the camera and see for yourself."

"Okay. This way."

They owned Las Vegas, the gangsters, the big corporations, and they could do a lot of damage, which I didn't want to deal with. I just wanted to find Elliot. As long as I could walk away with a bit of money, I would be content. So, I played along.

They marched me to the elevator, and the guard had to use a key to go up to the top. I was expecting a security room of some sorts filled with screens and controls, or an interrogation room, but it was a penthouse, grand and ornate and gaudy as the one I had seen in the movies. They told me to take a seat and wait.

I didn't sit down. I went to take in the view. Through the glass wall, the Vegas strip lit up like a golden river, cutting to the horizon. I scanned the horizon for that disturbance where Elliot was. The now familiar phantasms, haloes of animals, and, in the distance, columns of light shooting up to the clouds filled the dark sky, and the city hummed as if it were alive, a low hum which was suddenly disrupted by a helicopter landing on the rooftop. I saw the edge of its blade. I looked back at the guards, who began to fiddle with their earpieces as though they were readying themselves for actions.

Soon enough, the double doors sprang open, and in came a diminutive man, followed by an entourage of several people. He didn't have a hair on his head, or face. His nose was slightly crooked and his lips sinuous. His left eye was larger; it looked as though it was a camera portal. The ears and the chin pointed with a hint of menace. Altogether he resembled a turtle, and I recognized him instantly, the internet billionaire, Josh Baelz.

"Where is he?" Baelz hollered, looking about.

"It's an honor to have you, Mr. Baelz," one of the guards said.

"Where?" Baelz screamed.

The guard pointed to me. A man dressed in a black suit ran past Baelz and ran a scanner over my body, and then frisked me. After he was done, he turned to Baelz, "He's clear."

Baelz hollered again, "Please, clear the room!"

They retreated through the doors and closed them. Then, Baelz approached me with quick little steps.

"You must know who I am," Baelz said.

"I do. And?" I said.

He chuckled. "I have a proposition for you."

"Not interested," I said.

"Of course, you are. I can help you find him."

"Who?" I played dumb.

"Elliot Spinoza. Who else? I'm a big fan."

"What do you want with him?"

"I'm not going to lie to you. I want to apply his work. Make it practical. Make it widespread. Bring it to consumers."

"You want to bring Spinoza's equations to consumers?"

"I know. I know. It sounds ridiculous, right? But let's face it, everything is math, one way or another. You just have to know how to use it."

"Okay. If you say so."

"All I want is to meet Spinoza, to clear up a few things. That's all. Can you help me do that? Can you just let me know when you find him? After all you're the psychic," he said with a whiny little voice. And, for a moment, I could see him as a whiny little kid, who got bullied daily at school.

I stared at him in silence.

"We all know what you did for those little people," he persisted, smiling crookedly.

"Find him yourself. You're pretty good at finding people. You found me."

"You're easy. Just a little facial recognition. You know, what with the cameras everywhere. Especially here.

But. . . your friend is different. He's completely off the grid. My Lorrie hasn't picked up a whiff of him at all."

"Your woman?"

"No. No. My supercomputer. I called her Lorrie. She's been scanning the internet, all the cameras, an SWIFT for financial transactions. Nothing on your friend, but she picked you up. That's how I got here right away."

"Still not interested," I said. I flicked my index finger, and a thin lick of black flame swirled. I had the urge to put the black flame over his turtle head.

"I'll make it worth your while. Check this out," he said, and, turning to the door, he screamed, "Charlie!"

The doors swung open, and one of the men came rushing in, carrying a briefcase.

"Bring the case. Bring the case," Baelz said, waving his hand. "You're going to love this."

As the man approached me, Baelz ordered him, "Open it."

Inside the briefcase were neat stacks of money.

"Half a million," Baelz said. He picked up a stack and waved it in the air and threw it back. "All yours, Daniel. All you've got to do is let me know when you locate Spinoza. That's all."

"Not interested."

"It's hard cash. Hard to come by, but I've got a friend who will print all the hard cash I need. Pow, just like that. A load of cash," he said, punching the air.

Printed money from his crony. I was not interested. "I'm good."

"Don't tell me you're still loyal to him? I mean you guys were friends in high school, but that was before he married your girl. Isn't that right?" Baelz got close to my face. "I would say that your loyalty is misplaced. . . It's not like I'm going to do anything to him. I just want to buy his equations. Is that so bad? I just want to make him rich. Money is no object. I'm the richest man in the world." He handed me the briefcase. "No one needs to know."

He knew everything about me. Now, I really wanted to engulf his turtle head with the black flame and see what good his money could do for him, but then I thought about Cub and his shitty house. Cub could use the money. Of course, I would never tell Baelz when I did find Elliot.

"If you put it that way, thanks," I said. I took the briefcase.

"Excellent," Baelz said and turned to Charlie. "Give him a phone."

Charlie produced a cellphone from his pocket and handed it to me.

"Just press Call when you find him," Baelz said. "I'll make both of you rich."

"One more thing. When is the bomb going to explode?" I asked.

He thought about it for a moment and said, "It already did, just an hour ago. Our satellites was recording the whole thing. And nothing happened. It went out like a candle."

"Why?"

"To study gravity waves, of course." He gave me the official line.

Baelz extended his hand, and I did my best to shake it.

12

The desert didn't just end in the far distance at the foot of the mountain, it encompassed the very sense of vastness and everything in it. Different shades of brown wandered with the light and darkened next to the scrubs, the cacti, and the rocks, an extraordinary beauty in such a narrow variation of monochrome.

I was lost in the scenery as Cub drove. I hadn't slept at all last night, but my mind was as alert as if only five minutes had passed since our arrival in Vegas. The world was changing, and I was changing with it. Time and space seemed to have become a part of me, so that I passed with them and was not subjected to the change, as if I was no longer standing outside them or be ravaged by them. It was hard for me to understand and even more difficult for me to articulate.

Cub and I headed north, traveling across the desert, keeping in sight the disturbance in the horizon. We needed to get ahead of it and then cut across, or perhaps double-back to get to the source, where Elliot would be. I had no doubt of it.

"Where did the money come from again?" Cub asked suddenly.

"I told you. I got lucky at the table," I said. I had given Cub all my winning and Baelz's money. I didn't want to tell him about Baelz, and of course, I threw away the cellphone Baelz had given me.

Cub leered at me with suspicion, the same look he had given me when I had first told him.

"I don't feel good taking your money," he grumbled.

"You need it more than I do. I live in a nuthouse. What do I need a lot of money for? Besides, it's not my money. It belongs to the casino. You don't feel bad about taking their money, do you?"

"No. But you won it. It belongs to you now."

"No. I cheated."

"Really?"

"Yeah. I used my hmmm. . . ability. I could see the cards coming and the next number in the roulette wheel. Anyhow, I can always win more money if I ever need it."

Cub nodded and said nothing more.

He must have driven a hundred miles, north and

then east, until I saw that we were beginning to pass the darkened horizon. At the next dirt road, I told Cub to turn in. The road was relatively smooth at first, but soon enough it turned rough. The Mustang had to climb over a small rocky hill, and then descended into a dry riverbed. For a long stretch, it seemed as though the road had disappeared. "Keep going," I told Cub whenever he turned to me, with a faltering look in his eyes. We must have gone thirty miles and I was about to give up, when I saw that the air was almost purplish, and I could make out a hangar in the distance.

"There. See it?" I asked.

"Yeah," Cub said. He sped to it.

We stopped a hundred yards from the hangar; its tin roof had been painted sand color, an obvious attempt to camouflage it from the air. Tumbleweeds rolled down a nearby airstrip which was strewn with brown tarps. Obviously, whoever owned this place, they wanted secrecy. Could Elliot be here? I didn't know for sure, but I could see the purplish tinge of the air streaming up into the cloudless atmosphere like a beacon.

We got out of the car and looked around. The air was dry and hot.

"This isn't a good idea," Cub said. "It could be a drug-smuggling operation. If we show our faces, they'll have to kill us."

I thought about this for a moment and waved my left arm; seeing the black flame, I felt a little reassured.

"I think it'll be okay. You stay back at the car. I'll go and check it out."

"No, I'll go. I have experience with these things," Cub said.

"No, you stay back. I have to feel if he's here."

The ground was uneven, scattered with brown scrubs and weeds; here and there cacti stood serenely under the midday sun. I started hesitantly, observing, listening, and feeling as I approached the hangar. I could make out tire tracks and boots marks in the dirt leading inside. I came to a metal door and stayed still to listen. Indistinguishable voices echoed inside.

"Hello!" I yelled out and banged on the metal door.

The voices quieted, and the footsteps shuffled. I stepped away from the door, and in a moment, it opened a crack. An eye looked out, and then the door opened fully. A man came out with his right hand behind him; obviously, he was hiding a weapon behind his back. His face was sunburnt, etched with deep lines, and brutish. His hair was sandy like the color of the dirt and his clothes, a desert camouflage uniform and a flak jacket.

I put my hands up. "I'm sorry. I got lost. Can you give me directions? How do I get to Vegas?"

The man eyed the surroundings and walked toward me. In the hangar, I could see others.

"Is that your car?" he asked.

"Yes. I went off road. Sight-seeing. I've always wanted to see the desert. Then I got lost. Luckily, I saw the hangar."

"You're by yourself?" He flung his head in the direction of the car.

I turned to the car and saw that it was empty. Cub had hidden.

As I turned back to the man, I was struck in the stomach. I fell to the ground, breathless and in pain. From behind him, his right hand swung toward me, and a gun, a black Glock, pointed at my head.

"Who are you?" he said. "And don't give me that shit about getting lost."

"I'm a tourist. I told you. I just wanted to see the desert. Away from the crowds."

He grabbed my jacket around my neck and pulled me up. Standing behind me, he frisked me with one hand.

"Move." He pushed me toward the car with the gun against my back.

I could hear other men coming out of the hangar. I glanced back and saw three men; an older man was probably a leader, followed by two younger men, both carrying assault rifles. They stayed close to the hangar door as they watched.

I felt the man's muscular grip on my neck, the grip of a soldier. When we got closer to the car, I scanned for Cub, but I couldn't see him. I even pretended to stumble to make enough noise to let Cub know, and sure enough, the man screamed in my ear, "Get up!" My heart began to race, making it even more difficult to breathe. Strangely, I was more afraid for Cub. The man used me as a shield as he moved around the car, checking outside and inside the car, and then he looked all around the periphery.

"Open the door," he said.

I opened the door.

"Open the trunk," he said.

As I reached to pop the trunk, he said, "Slowly."

The trunk popped open, and he shoved me toward it. Inside the trunk was the briefcase lying its side.

"Open it," he said.

Going against my suggestion to leave the briefcase with the hotel, Cub had wanted to keep the money with him. It was understandable; after all it was more hard cash than he had ever seen in his life.

And it was all there, half a million from Baelz and the money from me.

"Woohoo! Jackpot!" the man yelled out. He got right into the case, taking out a stack and smelling it, as if he wanted to make sure the money was real. He had felt my body when he frisked me and probably judged that I was no match for him, and so he put the Glock inside his belt. He went for the money with both hands, ignoring me.

I took a step back. Pivoting my head slowly this way and that way, I tried to discern any trace of Cub. There was no sign of him. At least he was safe and hidden. By the hangar, the other men stood still as if they were waiting for a signal.

Flinging my left arm, I tried to make the flame bigger, to wake it up, but it remained the same. I couldn't wait anymore. I had to make a move while the man was still mesmerized by the stacks of money. I would have to grab his hair and hold it long enough for the black flame to engulf his head, and then I would jump in the car and drive away. But then suddenly the ground started to move. About ten feet away, the dirt shifted, and a big ball of tumbleweed started to roll off the rising mount of dirt. The head of a man, covered in dirt, emerged from the ground. It was Cub. In a flash, he leaped up and charged at the man from behind, slamming him against the car. Hundred-dollar bills flew into the air and scattered across the ground. Cub punched the man in the kidney, but the flak jacket shielded him. The man's elbow jabbed backward across Cub's face, and a fist followed. Cub fell on the ground. The man pulled his gun; Cub's foot swung up and struck the gun which went off with a bang and flew into a shrub. The man pulled a knife and jumped on Cub, who caught the hand holding the knife with both hands. The man put his weight into his arm, grunting, and pushed the knife's sharp point down, closer to Cub's neck. Cub's eyes were intense. As if repelled by Cub's gaze, the knife's sharp point seemed to stop. And then Cub's arms raised slowly, lifting the man off him.

I looked at the shrub where the gun should be, but I saw that other men from the hangar started to run toward us. We had to leave right away. My left hand enlaced the man's hair. I didn't know if the black flame would do anything, but the moment I touched his scalp, the part of the black flame jumped over his head, instantaneous, as if it was a hungry animal, and it dove into his head like the tentacles of an octopus. The man went limp and Cub shoved him off. The man lay flat on the ground; his eyes were unmoving and looking straight at the sky.

"We have to go," I told Cub.

Cub jumped into the driver's seat. I closed the trunk and went to the passenger side. As I touched the door handle, I heard the first loud bang from the assault rifle, and my legs flopped, unable to hold me up. I fell next to the car. A deafening salvo of gunfire followed, exploding in the desert sky. Bullets riddled the side of the car, shattering the window.

"Go. Go!" I screamed.

The car kicked up a plume of dirt as it sped off. I was glad to see Cub get away; he could still come back to rescue me later, if I was able to survive. I felt blood soaking my shirt. The bullet had cut through my back, through my spine paralyzing me, and had exited through my liver. Strangely, I felt not so much pain as fear. Instinctively, I pressed my hand over the wound to stem the blood. There was nothing more I could do, besides staring at the sky, which was slightly bluish with haloes of Pterodactyls gliding gracefully among the clouds.

The older man came into view; he stood over me. Four other men quickly came over, toting assault rifles.

"Frank, you take Scott and go after that son of a bitch," the old man commanded. His voice had a slight Southern drawl.

Two men promptly went off.

"What is going on with Henry?" the old man said as he approached Henry, who was a dozen feet away, and leaned over the man lying on the ground.

"What about him?" one of the men said, pointing to me.

"Look at him. You think he can go anywhere?"

"No, he can't. No, he can't," the same man said and laughed.

I raised my head and saw that the man, whose name apparently was Henry, hadn't moved at all, and that the black flame was flickering was over his head. The old man slapped Henry on the face and said, "Henry! Henry! Wake up, boy. What's wrong?"

The other men kneeled next to Henry and heckled him, trying to rouse him.

I was beginning to feel faint and tried to move my legs, but nothing. Suddenly, I noticed dark, earthen swirls, resembling snakes, squiggling out of the ground and passing right through my body, as though they were running from something. I pushed myself up and tried to crawl away, only to see that they were everywhere, thick as grass, as far as I could see, a gigantic expanse of energy snakes. There was no way I could get very far on my hands, so I lay flat and awaited my fate, though I felt that the energy snakes were doing something to me.

Abruptly, the old man stood up and came to me, growling. He grabbed my collar and yanked my face close to his. "What did you do to him?" the old man screamed, spewing foul breath thickened with the stink of cigar.

"Can't you see? He's lost his mind," I said.

"What? How?" the old man said, shaking his head as though he couldn't believe what he had heard.

I suddenly realized I could move my legs. And I no longer felt the pain. The swarm of energy snakes had restored me somehow.

"Tell me now," the old man said through clenched crooked teeth. His blue eyes were sharp and narrow, his face wizened, and his mouth snarling. He was obviously the leader, and I could see the venom and the will-to-power behind those eyes.

"You have Spinoza. Give me Spinoza and I'll give you back Henry," I said.

"Spinoza? Who are you?"

"Nobody."

"How do you know about Spinoza?"

"The whole world is after Spinoza. Give me Spinoza and I will give you back Henry and any amount of money you want," I said; images of Baelz's money flashed through my mind.

"Boys," the old man called out to the other two men. "Hold him down."

Each man held my hand to the ground and put their boots over my wrists.

"Boys, give me your knives," the old man said. "Spread out his palms."

The old man sat on my chest. His weight bore down heavily, making it hard for me to breathe, and he stabbed three knives into the ground, right next to my face. Then his lips drew up into a delightful smile as he plucked out a knife and waved in front of my face. "When I'm done with you, you're going to wish you'd never left your mama's womb. Ya going to wish you could crawl your way back into your mama's stinky hole." He leaned to my right hand and put the knife over in the middle of my palm and pushed down slowly. I screamed as the knife slid in.

The pain shot up my arm. My hand felt like it was being burned, and I jerked it reflexively, but the man's boot kept it pinned down. Blood swelled over my hand.

"Hah, you like that. Who are you?" the old man said. Seeing that I was grimacing and closing my eyes, he slapped me. "Look at me. I'll go on until you tell me."

He plucked out another knife and leaned to my left hand. The pain seemed to start even before the sharp edge cut through my palm. I howled. The old man chuckled and pushed the knife down slowly until the blade had gone all the way through. And as his right hand came within reach of the black flame, it jumped onto his hand. The old man jumped up and looked at his hand; his eyes were wide open and terrified. His right hand seemed frozen; the fingers curled in a claw. He shook it, but it wouldn't move, as though it had petrified. The other two men stared, their mouths hanging open, and they pointed their assault rifles at me.

"Ahhh," the old man muttered and sat down on my chest again. "What did you do to me?" He brought the claw in front of my face. With his left hand, he plucked out the third knife. "You're going to undo my hand and Henry and tell me everything I want to know." He stuck the sharp point to my cheek, just below the skin.

A wind suddenly picked up. But more than that, though the men couldn't see it or feel it, the ground began to stir, and an energy column shot straight up toward the sky, passing right next to me. "Ahhhhhh!" I let out a yell as I lifted my left hand, pulling the knife out of the ground, and flicked the black flame toward the energy column. Like lightning, it carried me up.

13

Earth became the size of a basketball within seconds. It was a ball floating in a fluidity of stars. An uncontrollable terror made me pull left hand from the red-hot energy column, and I began to fall back to Earth, tumbling fast this way and that, the Earth spinning through my field of vision. Air rushed past me, my clothes were nearly torn off my body, and the knives slid out of my palms. After a while, I caught sight of the California coast and soon the Nevada desert. I was plunging faster and faster. I was going to die. And if I was going to die, it was one hell of a way to go. My terror ebbed. I put out arms and began glide, and my body shot off at a straight tangent. I withdrew my arms and turned my body, and I went to another direction. After a few tries, I could fly here and there, effortlessly. Then the atmosphere thickened, and finally, some wisps of clouds passed by. An electric-blue Pteranodon appeared next to me. It was the same energy silhouette I had seen before; its wingtip scraped my arm, and it felt real, as if I had become the same substance as the electric ghosts. Turning to me, the creature squawked and dove away. I didn't know what was happening to me, but instead of fear, exhilaration, or nihilistic resignation, a clear recognition suddenly overwhelmed all my thoughts and senses: that everything was unreal.

I had to get back to down to Earth. I glided toward a Pteranodon and slammed into it. We tumbled together through the clouds, but I held on as hard as I could. When it finally spread its wings and steadied itself, I grabbed its neck. I made it dive toward the earth, as if it were a glider. Circling around the vast desert, we descended. In the distance was Las Vegas, and I kept the city behind me as I descended. At last, I saw it; Cub's car was speeding away. A Humvee was chasing after Cub, and sounds of gunfire rang out. I pushed the Pteranodon's beak down to get it to land where Cub was going, and I kicked it hard to go faster, but then it abruptly dropped vertically and stopped midair. My hands slipped from its neck, and it was as if I had been shot from a gun barrel, straight down.

I spread my arms and legs and could slow down a little. Still, I came in fast, hitting the ground and throwing up a plume of dirt. My body should have been crushed and shredded into pieces when I hit the ground, but I was whole. I stood up and shook off the dirt. The bullet wound through my liver had closed, my palms had healed, and all that was left to remind me I had not gone mad and imagined everything were the scars. Gunfire echoed through the sky. In the distance, Cub's car was speeding toward me, jumping over mounts of dirt, smoke billowing from the engine. Not far behind, the Humvee was gaining on it. I ran to intercept Cub, waving my hands. Cub turned hard and stopped right in front of me.

"Get in!" he screamed.

I jumped in, but he wouldn't go.

"Go. Go!" I said.

Abruptly the engine stopped.

"Get out. We're done for!" Cub yelled.

The Humvee stopped about a hundred yards from us. Two men got out and started to fire their assault rifles; the bullets pierced the car chassis with sharp metal pops. I crawled out, and Cub quickly followed me. We hid right next to the rear tire.

"How did you get here?" Cub asked, staring at me with wide eyes. "I saw you get shot."

My shirt was still red with blood.

"I caught a ride," I said. I raised my head a little and saw the two men kneeling by the Humvee as they continued to shoot.

"They're not coming just yet. They probably think we're armed," I said.

"They'll be on top of us soon."

I looked around. There were a few rocks around. I picked up two, the size of my fist, and gave them to Cub.

"You want me to throw rocks at them?" Cub said.

"Yes, when they come."

"Rock against gun?"

"Yes."

"They are not going to know what hit them."

I grinned at him.

Then I dug into the ground, and there it was, an energy snake, the same kind that I had seen earlier, the snakes that had moved through me. I put my left hand to the ground to take it into my hand. The most accurate description of what was happening would be that I absorbed the energy snakes through the black flame; I felt the energy bottling up inside me.

The gunfire slowed to a single pop at a time. I took a peek and one man was coming at us while the other held back at the Humvee and continue to shoot. I put my right hand on Cub, pushing the energy into him. He twisted and crunched as though he was rearranging his bones.

"He is coming at eleven o'clock. Make it count, Cub," I said. "I am going to distract them."

"Are you sure?"

"Yes. I was shot once already."

I peeked over the edge of the car and saw that he was close.

"Get ready," I told Cub and started to run away diagonally.

A burst of gunfire came from the man approaching us, and I dove to the ground. The man charged toward me, pointing his rifle. Suddenly, Cub jumped and threw a rock at the man. The rock literally blew across his arms, and the rifle landed ten feet away. The man fell to ground groaning. The man by the Humvee opened a burst on Cub, but he ducked down, hiding by the car. As soon as the burst of gunfire stopped, Cub hurled another rock at the Humvee. Even at that distance, it exploded through the windshield like a high-energy projectile causing the man to turn his face away. Cub sprinted to the rifle, leaping over the man lying on the ground, and took aim. A single shot rang out, and the man by the Humvee slumped to the ground.

I got up and approached the man on the ground. He glared up at me with a puzzled look; he was sweating, and his face was pale. Both of his forearms hung limply; blood was dripping from his sleeves.

"We have to patch him up," I told Cub.

Cub cut off the man's shirt sleeves and tied tourniquets around his biceps. The humerus and ulna bones in both forearms had broken and were showing through the skin.

"How many more are there at the hangar?" Cub asked him.

"Fuck you!" the man spat at Cub's face.

Cub wiped off the spit. In a flash, Cub's bare hand grabbed the man's arm where the bone was showing and squeezed. The man cried out; his legs kicked furiously.

"I'll ask you again," Cub said. "How many?"

"Fuck you," the man said. "I'm dead anyway."

"So be it," Cub said as he stood up.

I kneeled down next to him. "We'll be back and take you to the hospital," I said. The man just stared at me, unblinking. "I'm just looking for my friend, Elliot Spinoza." Still, the man said nothing, but an involuntary twitch of his face told me that Elliot was there.

Cub tied his legs together and set him against our car.

We took the Humvee and started for the hangar. Before we left, Cub checked the two assault rifles, changed the clips, and asked me if I knew how to use one. I told him I had shot similar rifles a couple of times before, many years ago.

The hangar looked too quiet. Cub stopped at a distance, and we got out. With the rifle scope, he scanned the periphery.

"Stay here. Close to the ground. Shoot when I give

you the signal. And keep shooting. Single shot at a time. Just point and squeeze the trigger."

"Okay. Don't kill the old man. I need him," I said and lay on the ground. I could still see the upper half of the hangar door, which was slightly ajar.

Pointing his rifle straight ahead, Cub moved low to the ground and fast. He must still have the energy I had channeled into him. He circled behind the hangar, but before he disappeared out of sight, he gave me the signal.

The first shot went off like a small bomb next to my ear. I aimed right at the door, which blew open, probably slammed against a wall, and bounced back. The whole side of the hangar began to slide open, and two men ran out and dove to the ground. I targeted one and squeezed. I couldn't see if I had hit him; immediately, I had to lie flat and keep my head down. They spotted my barrel flash. A salvo of bullets whooshed over my head. Without putting my head up, I raised the gun and fired another shot, and I kept firing. The whooshing came closer, and I had to crawl a few yards away. I put up the rifle in their direction and pulled the trigger. Suddenly, a cacophony of popping followed; it lasted a long time, but the firing in my direction eased. I kept firing blindly. At last, I heard I heard Cub yelling, "Clear!"

While I had kept them busy with my haphazard firing, Cub had entered the hangar from behind. He snuck up and knocked out the old man and killed the other two. The old man was still unconscious in the hangar. One of the two men was still oozing blood from a chest wound just above his Kevlar vest and lying very still, apparently dead; the other was gasping for air, his eyes unblinking, staring straight ahead. I leaned down to him and laid him on his back. I began to remove the Kevlar vest, but Cub put his hand on my shoulder.

"He can't be saved. The bullet penetrated his upper chest. Unless you can get him into surgery in the next fifteen minutes," Cub said coldly.

Cub was right. I shook the man and said, "Hey. Hey." Maybe, he would be conscious enough to tell me his last words, maybe to send word to his loved ones. He remained still.

With a splash of water, we roused the old man. He stirred, and when he came to, he immediately looked about with his narrow eyes, searching and mapping his environment, and identifying threats. He was clearly an experienced soldier.

I leaned over him and said, "Where is Spinoza?"

"Who are you?" he said with a slur. His eyes bulged out. "You flew into the sky. What are you?"

I smiled at him, glad that he was confirming what had happened to me, that I was not crazy.

"What is he saying?" Cub asked.

"How is it possible? What I saw," the old man said and looked about. "What did you do to my men?"

I ignored him. "Where is Spinoza?"

"You ain't getting anything from me."

"Tie him up, Cub. I'm going to search the place."

An airplane, a single propeller, sat in the hangar, which was large enough for four people. A small enclosure in the back housed an office and a kitchen. The floor was made of wood, and a thumping echoed underfoot as I moved about the enclosure. I searched in the corner and found a door in the floor. A whiff of stale air and urine rose from below, where a wooden staircase led down into the darkness. After a minute, my eyes adjusted, and I could see a mattress on the floor, a metal can serving as a urinal in the corner. Were they keeping Spinoza here? My throat felt as though it was choking up. They were trying to break him.

In the back of the hangar, where Cub had entered, the doors had slid open, and airplane tracks led to the airstrip. They must have flown Spinoza off. I beckoned Cub, and we went to the back to have a talk.

"How do we get the old man to talk?" I asked, keeping my voice low.

"I can try," Cub replied.

"You mean torture him?"

"Yes."

"He's experienced. He won't talk."

"We don't have time."

"Okay. Try but don't hurt him too badly."

I went back to the old man. Cub had tied his arms to a chair.

"Tell me where Spinoza is," I said somberly.

The old man sneered without saying a word.

"I see that you like knives," I said. I held up my hands in front of his eyes. Two scars ran the length of my palms. I saw that he tried his best to remain calm, but a terrified look crept over his face. "Give me a knife, Cub."

"I will do it," Cub said. He put his hand on my shoulder to move me out of the way.

"Spinoza is my friend. I don't want to put this burden on you."

"I'll do it. I'm trained for it."

"This is my burden."

"Let me do it."

"Understand one thing," I said to the old man. "I will torture every one of you until I find him." I stepped aside. Cub knew I was just playing the part.

"You're in control. Tell me when to stop, okay?" Cub said to the old man, almost sympathetically.

Cub held a knife in front of the old man. He put the dull edge to the man's right cheek and dragged slowly. Then abruptly he flipped and cut deep into the old man's face. A muffled cry escaped the old man's clenched teeth, and blood dripped down to his chin. Cub proceeded to cut the left cheek. The old man tried to jerk away, but Cub grabbed his hair and held him in place.

"You will bleed to death. Or you can tell me. This will end today," Cub said matter-of-factly.

There was a method to Cub's torture. He was cutting into areas supplied by different nerves to create maximum pain. He was cutting quietly, but the old man's screams reverberated along the tin roof of the hangar as if it was a cathedral.

Hearing the screams, I wondered if I had meant what I had said, that I would torture every one of them until I found Spinoza. Could I cut the old man up? Maybe I would as a payback for what he had done to me. I didn't even know I had it in me until I heard his scream; it sounded, somehow satisfying; this was perhaps part of the change that I was experiencing. For the first time, I was seeing things, including myself, as they were, not as they ought to be, disguised under a physical surface, or a moral cliché. What I had said about torturing every one of them sounded like a bluff even if I had the will to do it; after all, I hadn't seen my friend for over a decade. Hearing the screams, I knew I did mean it, not because of wanting to rescue Spinoza but of some bloodlust desires deep within me, the thirst for justice, which had been looking for a target. The scream sounded almost sweet, almost like an opera aria, one by Bizet, for the old man had gleefully stuck the knives into my palms and so he deserved it. But then, we all deserved it to some degree, all of us living in this world.

I went to the office area and searched the drawers, the files, the search history on the internet, anything at all to see if there was any clue about where they had taken Spinoza. I found nothing. I searched until the silence interrupted me. The old man had stopped screaming and had lost consciousness from either the pain or the loss of blood.

"What did you get?" I asked Cub. Fresh cuts littered the old man's face; they looked superficial, and the bleeding had stopped. His left eyelid had been peeled off, and the eye was unmoving.

"He's an experienced soldier. He'd die first," Cub said. He went to the sink and washed his hands.

I went outside to scan the sky. A purplish color flickered on the horizon, in the northeast. We would have to go in that direction. Suddenly, I remembered the man with broken arms.

I went to up Cub and asked him. "Cub, do you know how to fly?"

"Yes."

"Spinoza is northeast of here. We'll need to fly there."

"I'll check the plane," he said.

"What about the guy with broken arms?"

"I'll go get him first. It's not far from here. You can find the key."

"All right."

Cub set off with the Humvee, while I rummaged through the office. The key was in fact in the ignition. The plane had four seats, but the tank was only half-full. The old man and the man with broken arms would have to get themselves to the hospital. We could call for an ambulance after we left.

The old man was still out, and his shirt was covered with blood. I shook him, and his head flopped the other way.

"Hey. Wake up!" I shouted.

I pressed my finger to his carotid; he was cold. Now I could see a puncture wound right above his left clavicle. I got up. Just then, the Humvee came up. Cub got out by himself.

"Where is he?" I said.

Cub glanced at the dead old man and me and looked away.

"He's dead," Cub said and went to the airplane.

"Who?"

"They shot at us. They'd have killed us. They'd go for us again."

I knew it was true, but still, it shocked me; perhaps it was not the killing, but the fact that I was not prepared for it that shocked me. I was not prepared for what it took to satisfy my bloodlust. Whatever my reasons were, the final act would always require coldness.

I exhaled a long breath and said, "All right. Let's go."

We pushed the airplane out. Before we got in, Cub fetched the briefcase with the money from the Humvee, and he went about wiping all traces of us from the place. So, he hadn't forgotten about the money. He started the ignition, and as the plane ran down the runway, he said to me, "If it makes you feel any better, the coyotes got the other guy. They chewed him up pretty badly."

"No, it doesn't," I said firmly.

But it didn't make me feel any worse either.

14

The airplane lifted into the air and turned toward the horizon, at times dipping and tumbling as if it were a boat. Las Vegas was behind us, and Cub flew low to avoid detection and any potential trouble from the authorities.

The sun hovered in the sky, inching toward the horizon, throwing its pixelated rays over the purplish horizon. Below us, cacti poked skyward like fingers trying to reach heaven. A few clouds floated carelessly by, and the haloes of animals and the energy columns continued to fill the sky and were now as real to me as my own body. I might have enjoyed the scene, an idyllic, barren beauty, but the dead men we had left behind seemed to have given this world even more pseudo-reality. I did what I did to find Spinoza, but why was Cub doing this?

"Cub, are you not afraid of the cops going after us?" I asked him, speaking through the headset.

"No. They won't be able to connect us to those guys."

"How are you so sure? What about your car?"

"I burned it. It was built from scratch. No VIN. Nothing to connect me."

I scanned the horizon toward the west, and, sure enough, a faint haze of smoke hung in the far distance.

"You think of everything, don't you?"

"I was trained to. And until recently, I couldn't. Until I met you."

"What happened to you?"

Cub pushed the throttle; the airplane roared and bounced up and down as it rode strong air currents, but Cub held it in a narrow range.

"I caught something in Afghanistan. I'm not sure what."

He was not sure, but I was. I waved my left hand and the black flame came alive. It began to feel more and more like a living being, an angry animal of some sort, and if I were religious, I might even think it was a demon. It was Cub's demon, and now it was mine.

Cub began again, as though he couldn't contain himself, "It was after a raid in the mountains. We must have killed twenty fighters. The leader was wounded but still alive, and I questioned him. It must have been something I caught from him. After that, I was never the same. They transferred me back to Germany. The doctor thought it was PTSD. Everything became cloudy, like a nightmare, like something was sucking away my mind. Nothing mattered. Until you came. Things are clear now."

"Hmm, I am glad you're better," I said. "It must have the stress of war and the news of your family tragedy that tipped you over."

"What did you do to me? I felt so strong, like I'm superhuman."

"I gave you energy. Other than that, I can't explain it."

We flew for an hour, going higher and higher into the mountains. At last, I saw it, where the purplish sky appeared over a clearing on the side of the mountain. There, a compound made up of several houses scattered around a big central house, which stood imposingly on a manicured lawn. A landing strip started from the edge of the clearing and ended at a small hangar.

"Let's put it down," I told Cub.

"On the landing strip? They'll know we're here."

"Put it down," I said.

The airplane banked and then straightened. As it dipped closer to the ground, I saw a truck coming toward us from the main house. The truck ran alongside the plane as we landed. Once we got out, I channeled an energy column into Cub. "Get ready," I told him as his body flexed and chest expanded.

Two men kept their assault rifles on us as a third frisked us. He ordered us into the truck and took us to the main house.

For a mountain house, it was immense; the stone columns reached about thirty feet, and the door was at least half that height. The walls were also made of stone; in fact, the structure resembled a Bavarian castle. Inside, the interior gave an impression of opulence; a gigantic crystal chandelier hung from the ceiling and a wide staircase curved to the second floor. Portraits of old white men decorated the walls. The men led us through a hallway into a library. Bookshelves stretched to the ceiling on all sides. Behind a grand desk, an old man sat; he was dressed in a striped suit. His hair was gray, his face wizened, but his blue eyes locked on us with a piercing gaze. He was reading from a folder, which he closed and looked up at us. He looked familiar and famous; I had seen his face in a magazine somewhere but couldn't place it.

"Ahh, gentlemen," the old man said; his voice was slightly raspy. "I hope you've had a pleasant flight. Please, have a seat."

"Where is Spinoza?" I said tiredly. I sat down, put my hand on the desk, and toyed with a crystal ash tray. The library smelled of cigars and whiskey.

The three armed men stayed by the door, ready with their rifles.

"I see that you used my plane. What happened to my men?"

I gazed up at him but didn't answer; instead, I said, "Give me Spinoza and we'll walk down the mountain ourselves."

"You're that psychic? I've been briefed about you. Is that how you know where to find Spinoza or did a higher power put you up to it?" he said, leaned back in his chair, and gazed at me, as though he was trying to read me.

"I've had a long day. I'm not going to ask you again."

"I see you understand higher powers. These human powers can compel you to do things. I can see that. I see that you understand how important power can be," he said and kept his eyes on me. "I can also see your true colors, both of you. You're kindred with us. If only you could understand what we're trying to resurrect. More than resurrect! We will build a power that will last a thousand years. A power that will let our kind be at the top again, that will let us build new cities, new nations, a new world of order and glory, that will take us to space, that will let us create things yet unimaginable. More beautiful than anything that this insipid world can come up with. If you can see my vision, then you will join us."

"We are leaving here with Spinoza." I suddenly recognized him, John Kirch, another billionaire in this insipid world. He had inherited money from his father, who had profited from dealing with the Russian communists a hundred years ago and parlayed it into many more billions. His business empire fed off virtually every sector of the economy, from oil to high tech, and real estate to fine wine.

"The elements of confusion and dissolution which are making themselves felt in modern life, in the concept of life itself, and in the will to national self-preservation, cannot be eradicated by a mere change of those in office. The whole world must be built anew. We have the will, the resources, and the men. And now we have the power to defeat all our enemies. Unimaginable power."

"Power? How does Spinoza give you this power?" I asked. I had an inkling that Spinoza's equations could unlock some power and wanted to see if he would tell me more.

"You have no idea. You have no idea." John Kirch stared at me.

"Tell me then."

"It's far beyond my power to describe. Far more pow-erful than their gigaton hydrogen bomb. If you can only see it, you will open your eyes. It's incredible. The power can rip the earth itself apart. It's beautiful," Kirch said; his mouth slackened, and his eyes glazed over as though he was in a dream.

"So, you're not going to give me Spinoza?" I asked quietly and turned to glance at Cub.

"I haven't convinced you to join us, then?" Kirch said, raising his head to the three men standing behind us.

I knew that was the signal to kill us. John Kirch jumped up and ran to the backdoor, getting out of the way. I threw the ash tray to Cub and hopped over the desk. Cub caught the ashtray and broke it in half, and in a flash, he turned around and threw one piece at the man closest to him. At the same time, he ran toward the man. The piece of ashtray flew like a bullet; the sharp edge of the broken ashtray pierced the man's face, throwing him back on the floor; and his rifle went off, spraying bullets into the ceiling. The other two men aimed their rifles, but Cub was already halfway across the room. He let the second piece fly at the man in the middle; the sharp edge lodged in his shoulder, just above his flak jacket. Then, Cub was on the man on the floor; he picked him up, used him as a shield, and fired his rifle at the other two men. The salvo shredded their heads, which literally exploded as their bodies fell to the floor.

I looked to the backdoor. Kirch was gone. Without waiting for Cub, I ran after him. The backdoor led to a hallway. I followed the noises at the end, passing through several closed doors. From the hallway I could see that it was an armory; glass cages displayed rifles, shotguns, handguns, and knives. Kirch was standing in the corner and aiming a pistol at the door. As I saw him, he took a shot, but I pulled back in time.

"Your men are dead. Give up and you won't feel any pain," I called out, and I meant it.

"The rest of my men are coming. You will be the one who will feel pain," he growled.

I could hear the defiance and anger his voice. Then, the sounds of gunfire came from the front where Cub was.

"Do you hear that?" I said. "Call off your men before they're all dead."

"Who are you?" he said. Defiance and anger wavered; there was now unmistakable fear in his voice.

I took the chance and rushed into the room. He fired another shot; the bullet passed behind me, hitting the wall. I went at him, going for his gun. The moment my hand neared, a shot pierced my right palm and threw my hand back. I struck him across the chin with a left hook. He fell down and lay still. The pain was sharp but not nearly as bad as the knife. The blood poured out, then stopped. Wondering how the knife wounds had healed earlier, I examined my hand closely. The skin and the flesh inside began to crawl; the edges closed and sealed. And just like that, it was as if I had never been shot; only a rounded scar remained.

I picked Kirch up by his collar. Despite his all rhetoric about ruling the world, he was light and frail, an old man. I laid him in a chair, took off his tie, with which I tied his hands behind him, and bound his ankles to the legs of a chair with his own shoelaces. Then, I went to the glass cabinet and picked out a beautiful knife with a sharp edge and a pointed tip. Pulling a chair up close, I sat across from him and tried to wake him.

"Wake up," I said as I slapped his face. "Wake up."

After a few slaps, his head moved, and he came to. He took another couple of minutes before he became aware of his surroundings.

"My men will torture you just like your friend," he said.

"Really? Because that's what I am going to do to you. I guess you are right. We're kindred in that way."

"Spinoza. So delicate. All the brains in the world but no bronze. The way he screamed, it was almost sweet."

"You must be reading my mind. That was what I thought when we went through your men in the hangar."

"We? So, you didn't do it yourself. You got that dumb ape doing the dirty work. You have enough guts to carve me up?"

"Yes, he did. But now I'm going to enjoy your screams. Personally," I said so monotonously that it seemed to strike him mute. A glitter of fright flashed through his eyes.

"My men will carve you up."

"Shhhhh," I said and looked up to the ceiling. "You hear that?" He looked puzzled. "Nothing. All quiet. Either your men should be here already, or they're all dead." The gunfire had ceased a while ago, just before he woke up. Cub must have mowed them all down.

Kirch said nothing.

"We are going to set some rules before I begin. I'm going to keep going until you tell me exactly where he is, or until there is nothing left of you. I'm not going to bind your mouth so you can scream your sweet screams, but if you spit at me, I'm going to cut out your tongue. Agreed? Good." I held the knife's sharp tip to his cheek. "How many have you killed? How many have you tortured and maimed and robbed and disposed of? I demand justice. Let not appearance of age deter me. Let not mercy stop me. Let me reap justice for justice's sake." I pushed the sharp tip in his face. He jerked away. I grabbed his hair and held it in place just as Cub had done in the hangar. I pulled the knife an inch. He clenched his teeth, fighting with all his strength not to scream. Blood ran down his face. I pulled out the knife and jabbed his forehead. I carved him methodically, all over his face, just like Cub. Then his body shook, and he began to scream. But all I could hear was justice for justice's sake. The growling, howling, angry screams morphed into childlike cries. They were right when they said all men, if they lived long enough, would become children again. It was sweet. His fearful cries seemed to lift me higher and higher, like a masterful aria, giving purpose to my knife strokes as if orchestrating a masterpiece. Blood covered his face and blinded him as he whimpered. Justice, justice—that was all I could hear until a hand seized my wrist. Cub was staring down at me with alarm. Only now did I hear the words coming out of Kirch's mouth, "Downstairs. Downstairs."

"Oh," I uttered and stood up. Blood covered my hand. I had cut up almost every square inch of Kirch's face. Without saying anything more, I went out to the hallway to look for a bathroom.

I washed the blood off my hand. In the mirror, I saw myself as someone new, one not horrified by what he had done but more steadfast than ever in his belief. To be alive is to cause some portion of injustice. And for a man like Kirch, the injustice that he had been accumulating since his birth must have been enormous. He had deserved every slice of that knife.

Back in the armory, Cub had cleaned Kirch up as much as he could. Lines of blood clots crisscrossed his face, and Kirch seemed more settled.

"Let him loose," I told Cub.

With his arms and ankles freed, Kirch sat still as though he didn't know what to do.

"Call off the rest of your men," I said. "Or we'll kill them all, and you'll be next."

Kirch fumbled through his jacket and took out a phone. He dialed and, when someone answered, said curtly, "Everyone stands down. Understood?" The man on the phone replied, "Yes, sir."

"Take us to Spinoza," I said.

A trapdoor behind the display of guns led down a stairway into a subterranean tunnel. It was well lit by lightbulbs hung at intervals of six feet, and it had an earthen, mildew smell. We followed behind Kirch. With the barrel of his rifle, Cub would poke him in the back now and then, just to remind him. We passed by a cavern filled with bottles of wine, which were without questions very expensive; I had once read an article about Kirch's wine collection worth hundreds of millions. I wondered when Kirch would have time to drink them all. Abruptly, Kirch stopped and leaned against the wall. No doubt, he had lost too much blood. Cub took him by the arm, but Kirch seemed to regain his composure and shook him off. He started off again.

We passed by several closed doors and turned a corner.

"Stand down," Kirch said as we came to a guard.

The guard looked baffled as Kirch came into his view.

"Open the door," Kirch said.

The guard punched the code in the keypad. The metal door popped open. Unable to contain myself, I rushed in.

Elliot Spinoza sat at the small table with a pencil in hand, scribbling his equations under a moribund lamp. The room was like a small prison cell; a small bed sat against a black wall. In the far corner were a toilet and a sink. Though he appeared older, his dark, slightly curly hair framing his face, the wide earnest eyes, prominent nose, and seemingly perpetually smiling lips were the same as those of the thirteen-year old boy I had first met. "Daniel!" He jumped up and embraced me.

"Did they hurt you?" I asked.

"Not so bad."

Emotions of all sorts overcame me—sadness, regrets, but also happiness. Elliot was good. I should have never distanced myself from him because of Margo. I had been so wrong.

"Let's get you out of here."

"You found my notebook. I've always believed in your ability," he said breathlessly.

"Yes, I did. Let's go."

Just then the guard fell down on the ground. Cub had struck him behind the head. "Just in case," Cub said.

Elliot turned to them. "Who are they?"

"Cub is with me. You know John Kirch already. I made him cry the way he made you." I pulled Elliot along. "I ought to kill this son of a bitch."

We retraced our steps. In the armor room, we halted

as Cub loaded up on weapons. I also armed myself with a rifle. Elliot said he didn't know how to fire a gun.

"Kirch," I said, staring into Kirch's eyes. "We're going to go out there. We're going to take the plane. You're going with us. We will let you off when we land. If anything happens, I'll kill you first. Then I'll hunt down your family and cut them up and then kill them. One by one. Even your little great grandkids. All of you. Understood?"

"Understood," Kirch said.

"All right. Let's go," I said.

Cub used Kirch as a shield, pushing him along. Elliot was in the middle, and I was at the end as I had to watch our backs. Steadily, we moved through the library and had to step carefully, as there were dozens of bodies strewn among pools of blood. The smell of blood saturated the air. I was shocked to see the carnage. It should be clear to Kirch not to try anything with us.

Outside, a platoon of Kirch's soldiers greeted us with their rifles.

"Stand down. Stand down!" Kirch screamed hoarsely, and he was shaking.

The soldiers lowered their weapons, and we went to a truck.

"Tell them not to follow us," I told Kirch.

"Don't follow!" Kirch screamed again.

We got into the truck and drove to the airfield. We got into the same airplane we had arrived in. Cub was glad to see the briefcase with money still there. Cub and Elliot went up front. I sat in the back with my gun pointing at Kirch. Now and then I had the urge to shoot him in the head and throw him out of the plane.

15

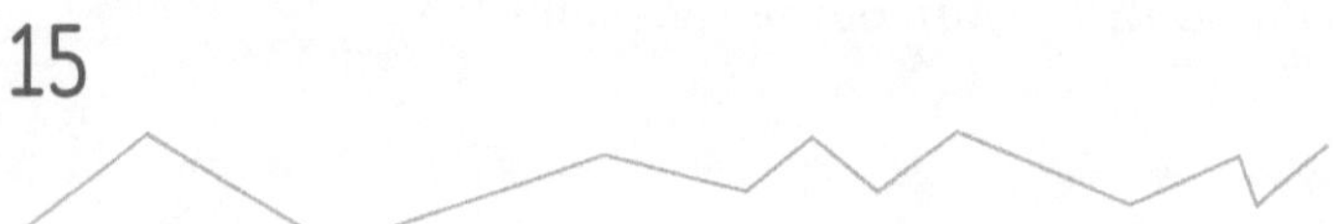

Cub flew back to the same landing strip so we could let Kirch off. He landed and took the plane all the way into the hangar. Things hadn't changed; the blood-soaked body of the old man was still slumped on the ground, and a swarm of desert flies scattered. The air had a blood-tinged smell. Kirch got out and sat in a chair, looking ahead vacantly. I didn't want Elliot to see the dead man, so I took him to the Humvee. Soon Cub, the briefcase of money in hand, joined us.

"You didn't kill Kirch, did you?" I asked Cub as we drove away.

"No," he said quietly. "Why would I? I had no reason to."

"All right. I just want to make sure."

"I only do what's necessary."

"Okay. I'm sorry I asked."

It was then that I noticed a strange forlorn look on Elliot, as if he didn't know where he was. The Humvee rumbled and rocked over the desert terrain. The sun was near the horizon and cast a reddish hue over the sky which was streaked by electric haloes and energy columns.

"Are you okay, Elliot?" I asked.

He turned to me and wrinkled his forehead as if he couldn't understand.

"Are you okay? You may be in shock. . . hmm. . . because of what you saw."

He blinked and looked at me, perhaps wondering.

"How are you not, Daniel?" he said at last.

"I'm nuts as you know."

He laughed.

"I live in a nut house now. A permanent resident of the McFadden Psychiatric Institute," I said.

"How did you end up there?"

"A long story. But I've been reading about you. The youngest recipient of the Field Medal. Solutions to this and that equation. I'm very impressed to say the least. But we all knew you would achieve great things."

He grew pale as if he just remembered something. He said, "Where's Margo?"

"She's back in LA," I said and cringed. Cub also threw me a weird look. I didn't know if Elliot could handle the truth, especially if I were to tell him that Margo was in a coma, that an invisible spiderweb now encased her head, or that I was probably the only one who could remove it.

"Good," he said. "I'll have to call her when I have a chance."

His voice was as I remembered it, a little high and clear. He spoke so casually that I thought he must be in shock and was unable to understand the gravity of the situation.

"This is Cub. He has been helping me," I said, suddenly remembering that they hadn't been introduced.

"It's an honor to meet you," Cub said.

"Thank you for coming," Elliot said.

"Where should I go?" Cub asked when we got to the main road.

The sun was setting.

"We can't go back to Las Vegas. They'll be all over us," I said and turned to Elliot. "Maybe we should stay clear tonight and decide. We need to go over the details first." It was all up to Elliot; I would tell him everything and let him decide. To gauge the situation, I asked Elliot, "Did Kirch get what he wanted from you?"

"I gave him the equation," Elliot said.

"Good. Then he won't be coming after us."

"With a couple of mistakes," Elliot said and laughed. "There are only a few people in the world who could figure them out, and it will take them a while."

"Hmm. So, he might still come after us. . . I should have put an end to him."

"I don't think he really knows what it can do," he said.

"It's settled then. We have to stay clear of Las Vegas and make our way back to LA as discreetly as possible. We'll need to hide you, Elliot, and we'll get Margo. Then we'll figure out how both of you can disappear. Or however else you want to play it. If you want to give the FBI your equation, it's entirely up to you. Maybe that is the best way. Only the government has enough resources to protect you, if you trust it."

Elliot nodded. "I'll think about it."

"Whatever you decide, I'll be there to make sure you're safe."

"Thanks, Daniel."

Cub stopped by a roadside market, El Ranchito, where the truckers frequented. We bought food, water, firewood, and serapes. We would tough it out in the desert for the night. I would never turn Elliot to the FBI, but I needed to figure out a way to get Margo.

We drove offroad, over some rough terrains, and finally, we headed down into a canyon hidden from all sides. As the sun set, the land became increasingly dark and surrounded by a rim of reddish and pale blue sky. It was a moonless night and the stars began to appear. A coyote howled now and then. Cub started a fire, and we sat around eating sandwiches in silence. In the still air, the smell of desert dust mixed with the scent of burning pine, and it was truly soothing. Cub passed around a bottle of rum; it was cheap and tasted awful, but it seemed to calm us all the same.

"Elliot and I have been friends since high school," I told Cub as a way to break the silence after we finished our sandwiches. "And Margo. The three of us were inseparable. . . I'm happy that you and Margo got married."

"Hmm," Cub grunted.

"How is your father, Elliot?" I said.

"I haven't talked to him for five years. He wanted me to join his firm," he said and sighed. "He wanted me to put my equations into his machine. To do what? To collect dollars from the stock markets. Every seconds of every day. What is the point? I told him I wouldn't trade all the dollars in the world for my Fields Medal. I told him that his life was like a beetle rolling a ball of dung up the hill. He hit me. We haven't talked since. None of my family would talk to me since. Or rather, I wouldn't talk to any of them. What is the point?"

"It would be better if you had kids. They'll come around once they see the kids."

Elliot laughed. "Not anymore. Not the way I am. Not in this world."

"What do you mean?"

He looked at Cub for a moment, perhaps uncertain if he could trust Cub, and then he said, "Either the world is not what it seems, or I'm losing my mind."

"What happened at your house? Were you there two nights ago?"

"No, why? What happened?"

"Margo asked me to come. When I got there, it seemed as if a part of the house was missing. As if someone had cut through it with a razor." I wanted to tell Elliot about my visions, seeing the flows of energy and the electric haloes of dead creatures floating in the air, but I felt it was not the right time.

"It must be Margo. She was probably putting it together," Elliot said, looking ahead vacantly as if he was speaking to himself.

"Putting what together? Your equations?" I asked.

"Do you have my notebook?"

"No, I lost it."

"No matter. I will show you tomorrow. If my calculations are correct, the earth is moving away in space in the morning."

"Uh huh," Cub grunted.

I knew Cub couldn't understand, and I didn't understand either. "I don't understand," I said.

"Let me explain," Elliot said. "So, the Earth is orbiting the sun. But the sun is also orbiting the center of

Milky Way Galaxy at about five hundred thousand miles per hour. Tomorrow, from around three to nine in the morning, we should be in a position on the earth's surface where it's moving away from space. While on the other side, where it's dark, the earth's surface is moving into space. It should be safe for me to demonstrate."

Cub wrinkled his forehead and shrugged. I thought I understood.

"Is that why everyone is after you? The FBI is after you. Josh Baelz is after you. Foreign governments are after you. Kirch is after you," I said. I knew we had to lay out the details sooner or later. "What kind of power can it have?"

"You will see," Elliot said.

I would have to wait. There was much that I wanted to say to Elliot—how sorry I was that I had shunned him even as he and Margo had gone looking for me-but, as usual, I kept quiet. At least now I could reach out and put my hand on his shoulder, knowing that my friend was here. Nothing could be more real than that, nor more comforting. Then we fell into silence. Elliot took out a pencil and paper and began to scribble his equations.

The fire was fed through the night. I could hear Cub waking up and moving about. He slept with his rifle next to him. The starry night sky was filled all sorts of energy, colors, and haloes of prehistoric animals, though I was sure that only I could see them.

16

A distant rumbling must have woken Elliot.

"Someone is coming," Elliot said as he shook me.

Cub and I jumped up.

Scarlet sliced through the distant horizon, the leading edge of the sunrise. Against the still darkened landscape, we saw the flickering of headlights. Within a minute we had gathered our things, and we bolted along a ravine with the headlights off. The grayish early morning light was enough for Cub; he drove very fast, at times swerving the Humvee abruptly to avoid boulders. I was in the passenger seat and Elliot in the back, both of us holding on to steady ourselves against the violent jumps of the car. Suddenly, the span of the desert opened up wide. Here, the Humvee could speed up, and it kicked up an enormous plume of dust. I knew they could see us and were coming for us. If we could get to the highway, we could blend in with traffic. I looked back but couldn't see the headlights following us anymore. The sky was getting steadily brighter. Maybe we'd really made it. I thought we should go north; we could get to Reno and disappear from there.

"Let's get to the highway," I said.

Cub nodded with a grunt.

Suddenly, the ground exploded twenty yards in front of us. A missile ripped the ground. The Humvee skidded and fell into the crater; it flipped over and rolled several times.

When I woke up, my ears were ringing loudly. The windshield had shattered. Hanging upside down from my seatbelt, I felt blood oozing from a cut in my forehead and dripping to my hair. Cub was outside, and he couldn't open the door because the roof was dented, and the edge of the door had sunk into the ground.

"Close your eyes!" I heard him scream.

He bashed the window with the butt of his rifle. He cut the seatbelt and helped me out of the car. Pain was pulsing in my neck. My first instinct was to check on Elliot. Probably because of his weaker constitution, he was still out, though I didn't see any outward injuries on him. As Cub got him out and tried to rouse him, I scanned the horizon. The plumes of dirt in the distance could only be the enemy convoy coming at us. In the sky, I caught the briefest glint of the rising sun against a drone, which must have fired a missile at us. Apparently, they hadn't wanted to kill us.

"We have to move!" I screamed at Cub. There was a hill along way toward the left, but Elliot remained unconscious and lay still on the ground. "Cub, we have to move."

Cub picked up Elliot and put him over his shoulder, and I carried the rifles. We ran as fast as we could, which was more like a slow jog. After twenty yards or so, Elliot woke up. He got down, sat on the ground, and held his head.

"Elliot, can you walk? We have to go," I said.

"What happened?" Elliot asked.

"C'mon," I said, trying to pull him along. "We got shot by a missile from a drone. The car flipped over. You passed out. They're coming. We've got to go."

Elliot just sat on the ground as if he was wondering about something.

"Elliot, pull yourself together. We've got to go!" I screamed.

"Go where? This is the desert. There's nowhere to go. The drone is watching us," Elliot said with an uncanny clarity to his voice. He got up and started to walk back to the Humvee.

"What are you doing?" I hollered.

"I've got a better solution."

"What? Turning yourself in to them, Elliot? We've got to get out of here," I said. I grabbed his arm and pulled him back.

He turned to me, stood still, and looked me in the eyes. "Trust me. Trust me," he said softly.

I held his arm tightly, but there was something in his voice. I let him go.

Clearly, he had been shocked out of his mind. He raced toward the Humvee. Cub stood still and shrugged. Whatever was to happen, I could never leave Elliot, I knew that now. I ran after him.

Elliot crawled into the car. When he got out, he had two pieces of paper, one in each hand.

"Can we go now?" I said.

"We can't outrun them, Daniel," he said.

"What do you want us to do?"

"We wait for them," he said very calmly.

Cub went between us and took position in the crater made by the missile. The crater was at least twenty feet wide and six feet deep at its center. Of course, he fetched the briefcase with the money and set it at the bottom of the crater. Cub checked the rifles and set down the cartridges.

"Cub, you don't have to be here. Make for the hills. We'll hold them off," I said.

"Get ready. They're coming," Cub replied.

Beside the upturned Humvee, the desert landscape around us was flat and desolate. There was not even a rock anywhere to hide. As I looked at the hill in the distance, which was rounded and smooth, I now realized the chance of hiding there was slim. Reluctantly, I jumped into the crater as well. Cub gave me a rifle and two cartridges. I wasn't afraid for myself; I was terrified for Cub and Elliot. I had survived being stabbed and shot through the liver, and I knew I would survive this, but what about them? There was only one thing I could do. I searched around frantically for a flow of energy. I dug into the ground with my bare hands.

"What are you doing?" Cub said.

"Remember how you got stronger when I touched you?"

"Yeah."

"That's what I'm looking for."

A blue channel, like water, flowed underground, glittering with sparks. I put my hand with the black flame into it and felt it flowing through me. I tapped Cub, and he closed his eyes and grunted and stretched his body as if it were expanding. Elliot was next; I turned around expecting to see him, but instead, he was still standing above the crater and looking toward the advancing convoy with almost an expectant and excited look.

"Elliot, get down here! What are you doing?" I yelled.

Without taking his eyes off the horizon, he got in. I put my hand on him, but he felt nothing. He continued to gaze at the convoy with boyish excitement. My heart dropped; how were we going to protect him? I had no idea why the energy flow worked on Cub and not Elliot.

"Stay in the hole, Elliot," I said.

Holding the two pieces of paper in his hand, he didn't seem to hear me. The pieces of paper were scribbled over with math, half of the equation written on one piece of paper and half on the other. Maybe Elliot was going to negotiate our freedom with the equation.

At last, they arrived. The convoy looked like a small army, with at least ten Humvees, ten jeeps and trucks, and six dirt bikes. They were filled with men in army fatigues, fully armed. There were machine guns mounted on the Humvees. They stopped about fifty yards from us. The men disembarked and scattered into positions on the ground.

"Come out with your hands up!" came the command from a loud speaker mounted on a Humvee. I recognized the voice, raspy but deep and haughty. It was John Kirch.

"I should have killed that son of a bitch," I said.

"Come out with your hands up. I am giving you till the count. . ."

A shot ran out. Cub had taken a shot, which shattered

the speaker. Immediately, we all ducked down as a hail of bullets washed over us. As the bullets hit the overturned Humvee behind us, it sounded like it was raining on metal, and my heart was thumping in my ears, all too disorienting.

"Good shot, Cub." I patted him on the shoulder. I turned to Elliot and was about to reassure him, but instead, I saw that he was smiling. His face was almost giddy as if he was a boy playing hide and seek.

The firing stopped.

"They are coming," Cub said.

"Let's take them, one by one."

"When it's time, I will make a run for it. We need to take out Kirch," he said.

"Yeah, sounds good."

Just then, Elliot rose with his hands in the air.

"I am coming out. Don't shoot!" Elliot shouted.

"What are you doing? Get down here, Elliot!" I yelled. I jumped toward him but missed as he got out of the hole.

Elliot glanced at me with an impish look, jovial and happy. "I have to do it now. There is no more time," he said.

He took a couple of steps.

"No. No!"

"Watch this," he mouthed to me. He must have gone mad. At that time, I had no idea what he meant; only in retrospect do I now know that what he was about to do was, without doubt, the most significant thing in the history of mankind.

Elliot walked toward them slowly, raising his hands high and holding a piece of paper in each.

"Get back here, Elliot!"

I peeked over the edge. The sun was rising higher, and it was a scary sight. There were at least a hundred men scattered about. They all had their gunsights on Elliot as he walked toward them.

At that moment, the staccato chop of machines came from the right, from the flat expanse of the desert. In unison, Kirch's men turned to it; some of them scrambled and got out shoulder-fired missiles. Three helicopters appeared, and on the ground a row of Humvees and jeeps was speeding toward us. The helicopters flew over us and started to circle. They were Apache helicopters and painted black.

Suddenly, far above us in the clouds, the drone exploded into a fireball, and debris rained down, streaking smoke. Chaos erupted. Three shoulder-fired missiles took off. The two Apaches directly above us were hit, and one burst into flames and crashed. The other took off with a huge trail of smoke. The third Apache evaded, and its gun lit up, tearing up the men on the ground. The machine guns on the Humvees opened up on the helicopter, and two more missiles went off. The Apache shot up high into the sky as it dropped flares behind it. From the right, from where the row of Humvees and jeeps was coming, bullets started to fly. Kirch's men returned fire. The continuous gunfire was deafening.

I was watching the battle as if it were a movie; I was watching the Apache as it fled to the horizon and thought that this was our chance to get away. Abruptly, Elliot came into my view; he was still standing there, fully exposed. "Elliot, get back!" I screamed and jumped out of the hole. He turned back to me and said, "I have to do it now. The earth is moving out of position. Watch this." His hands were holding the pieces of paper upright so that I could see the scribblings.

Then it happened.

A bullet struck Elliot's left knee. He fell. And as he fell, his hands came together. The two pieces of paper aligned. The equation was whole. The paper became a void, a round black nothingness. It expanded and everything in its way became nothingness, too. It expanded at an incredible speed and flew across the desert westward and upward into the sky. It was a round black hole that gobbled a quarter of the sky before it disappeared into outer space.

Kirch's little army vanished—Humvees, jeeps, guns, men, the Apache flying in the sky, along with part of the ground. The few men who were lying on the ground remained, though they lay very still, and I could see white webs encasing them, the same as Margo. There were other things left, the lower legs of the men who were at the periphery of the void and pieces of their weapons, and parts of the vehicles; it was as if a razor had cut clean through everything.

And Elliot had vanished.

17

Elliot's equation was the most powerful weapon humankind had ever known, not the atomic bombs, just mathematical symbols. Even an atom bomb could only re-order matter, but Elliot's equation could rip the fabric of space and annihilate all matter in its path. How was it possible?

That was why everyone—all the governments, and billionaires, like Baelz, Kirch—was trying to get it.

I was beyond shocked. Despite the paranormal things I had experienced up till then, I was not prepared for this. I was standing there, staring at what was left of Elliot, his lower legs. There was no bleeding, just shoes and jeans covering the stumps, and everything above the knees had simply disappeared.

He had meant to put the pieces of paper together in the other direction so that the void would move away from him, but the bullet to his knee had brought the papers together unexpectedly, causing the void to appear with Elliot in its path.

A row of Humvees and Jeeps stopping right by the hole shook me out of my shock. I looked up, as if I was in a dream. The vehicles were all painted black, and men in black uniforms poured out. Apparently, they were far enough from the void and had been spared. What's more, the void had annihilated all of Kirch's men.

"Don't fight them, Cub," I said. There were too many of them, and I wanted to know who was behind these men.

Cub threw down his rifle. We got out of the hole, and they put handcuffs on us and told us to wait. The men then scattered and went about gathering everything around, the remains of men, equipment, and guns that had been cut by the void. Soon a transport helicopter landed, and they took us to it.

From the air, I saw the path of the void. A gouge in the earth of at least a few hundred yards, long and wide. I wondered what would happen if the void had gone the other way, directly into the earth.

The helicopter flew directly north over the vast expanse of the desert and finally descended. From the air, the complex looked like a rocky hill, but as the helicopter landed, I could see that the structure had been built right into the rocks. The helicopter took off as soon as we were taken out. A couple of guards guided us with their rifles pointed at our backs through a door camouflaged as a slab of rock. Inside, it was darker and noisy with machines and men working. The air smelled of dry dirt, chemicals, solder.

They loaded us on a tram that wound along a large tunnel, which curved in a circle. A tube ran the length of the tunnel, punctuated with stations equipped with monitors and men working around them. The contraption reminded me of the CERN particle accelerator. The tram finally stopped. They took us into an elevator and went up. The elevator opened to living quarters that must have been for someone important, with its luxurious leather couches, sleek glass tables, and light sculptures hanging from the high ceiling. The air was clean and filtered. On the wall hung a large screen, and on the opposite side was a glass wall, framing a sweeping view of the desert. The guards took off the handcuffs and pointed us to the couches. We sat and waited. Cub seemed to be studying the surroundings and gauging the guards. I knew he still had all the energy I had channeled into him; we would wait for our chance.

"Hey, hey," a voice rang out loudly as the door in the far side of the room opened.

It was Josh Baelz, the billionaire turtle man. His bald head shone as though it had recently had a new coat of wax. Dressed in a tan sweater and jeans, he might be mistaken for the help. "So, you found him," he went on. His eyes widened and glazed like a mad man. "Where is he?"

I couldn't get myself to answer. Had it really happened? Had Elliot just disappeared? Maybe I had hallucinated the whole thing just as I had been seeing all the electric haloes, or the black flame on my left hand. I closed my eyes, hoping that I might be back in the asylum.

Baelz went to the window and gazed out at the desert.

"You know, I love the desert. This is one place where you can do something great. There is space for your mind to roam. You can build shit here. And the best part is that it's so vast and barren, that it lets you know upfront," he said, shaking his head, "that you can't mess up. Because if you do, you're dead." He turned to us. "So where is Spinoza?"

"He's disappeared," I said monotonously. For the moment I was mesmerized by his bald head, imagining myself carving it up, just as I had done with Kirch. Strangely, I found it pleasurable even to imagine it that I was smiling.

"What are you smiling about?"

"I said, he disappeared."

"Actually, I'm just messing with you. I already knew that. Here look at this," he said. Baelz turned on the screen and showed a view of the battle. "It's one of my satellites. I saw the whole thing. They took out two of my helicopters. That was pretty good. The idiots flew them too close, and then the black void. It blew my mind."

The view was from space. Baelz zoomed into the hole in the ground. And there we were; Cub and I were crouching in the hole, while Elliot was standing outside it. He forwarded to the moment when Elliot got hit in the knee and the void appeared. He zoomed into the void. It was the blackest of black that I could ever conceive, perfectly uniform, perfectly black.

"Wow. Look at it go," Baelz said with zeal. "Now check this out."

He showed us another satellite image, following the void as it shot into space.

"Amazing, isn't it? Actually, it's all about perspective, don't you think?"

"What is?" I asked.

"Anything. But in this case, motion. You see, it looks like the black thing was flying through space, but the thing is that we are, or more precisely, Earth is moving. The earth is revolving on its axis at 1,000 miles per hour. It's moving around the sun at 67,000 miles per hour. But that's not all. The earth and the sun are whirling around the center of the galaxy at 490,000 miles per hour. So, you see, we were moving away from it. If the earth had not moved, the Void would have cut the earth in half. The only thing the black void was and still is doing is expanding. It's incredible. It's growing exponentially. Soon, it will slice through the universe. What's more, the black void came into existence on Earth, but it has none of Earth's momentum. It defies all laws of physics."

"How?" I was stunned. This was what Elliot had tried to explain to us the night before, but now seeing it for myself, I found it more understandable.

He stood still and stared at me. Then he said in a soft voice, "I don't know yet."

"It came from Spinoza's paper," I said.

"Yeah. Maybe it's a doorway to parallel universe."

"What are you saying?"

"It's only a hypothesis."

"Okay," I said.

"Yeah. We can't prove anything yet, but we are working on it."

"You and who else?"

"Oh, a bunch of us. But mostly me and Munsch," Baelz said.

"You see, from what I've seen, more precisely, what you are capable of, Daniel, and what the black void is capable of, I'm more convinced than ever. There is only one reason that you or the black void could defy the laws of physics, Daniel. Occam's razor, right? Not that you possess superpower. No. Not that you're a psychic. No. There is only one reason." He went to the glass wall and looked out. "This is extra-dimensional stuff."

"What?"

"I'm still working it out."

I didn't reply.

"Check this out," Baelz said and showed us another satellite recording, this time of me lying on the ground with the old man sticking knives into my hands, and then of me flying upward into the sky. "You see. How did you defy gravity? Superpowers like Superman? No. A better answer is that there is an extra-dimensional force working here. Munsch thinks we have a parallel universe. That's why he convinced me, and we exploded that gigaton hydrogen bomb next to the sun. He wanted to punch a hole in space, and then escape from this universe through this hole. But now. . ." He looked at me. "Everything changes now. The black void is our way out. Even if we can't go through it, we can harness its power. What if we can shape it and direct it. It would be the most powerful weapon ever. It can negate nuclear weapons. That's what Kirch was going after. If he had gotten it, he would create the Fourth Reich."

"The briefcase of money. That was how you tracked us." I leered at Cub.

"When I got a whiff of this, I didn't know what to make of it," he said, ignoring me. "Military satellites caught images of the black void twice before. Once, a few years ago, in the mountain. It turned out that was the first time was when Elliot Spinoza discovered the equation. The Void Equation, that sounds about right." He chuckled. "They didn't know where it came from. We were lucky that the earth was in the right configuration. The second time was a few days ago at Spinoza's house. Then it was obvious that Spinoza had something to do with it. We went back to the mountain incident, and sure enough, Spinoza's cabin was also damaged the first time. That was when I told them to bring you in, but. . ." he waved his hand in the air. "I couldn't trust the FBI. I want the power for myself. Hence the cash. Not your fault. Not too many people can resist cold hard cash. And you should thank me; I told those FBI brutes to lay off you guys."

Baelz went behind the bar and poured three glasses of whiskey.

"That brings us to where we are. So, Daniel, now you know everything. Please give me the equation or Void Equation as I like to call it. Once I figure out the whole thing, I guarantee you and your friend will be rich beyond your wildest dreams. In fact, I will give you each, say, fifty million for the Void Equation. That's a bit too much cash to carry, but I can transfer it to any bank you like. What do you say?"

I needed a drink. I took the drink from the bar and went to the glass wall. I downed it, and it felt good going down. It was past noon, and the desert took on a homogenous bleached brown glare under the sun. Beautiful in its own way.

Cub hadn't said anything; he sat there and watched the guards, probably thinking of ways to kill them. With the energy still stored in Cub, he could take the guards easily. Glancing at Cub, I knew I would have to act soon. I knew that Baelz's song and dance was to soften us up; he would kill us the moment he got the Void Equation. I would never give Baelz the equation even if he were to keep his word; I would never give the ultimate power to the Turtle Man. Conjuring it up in my mind, I could see each letter, each mathematical symbol of Elliot's equation, as if the image in my brain were a page from Elliot's notebook. I scrutinized it in my mind, but the barrenness of the desert intruded. Time to carve up the Turtle Man. I held him responsible for Elliot's death. If he hadn't shown up, if he hadn't been so hungry for power, Elliot would still be here.

What was it about men like him? All they wanted was power, regardless of the hell that comes along with it. But then again, they were all the same, Baelz and Kirch, and they deserved justice more than anyone. I was going to enjoy it. I turned around and, abruptly, things went blurry. I fell to my knees as a column of electric fire zapped from behind the counter. Baelz was holding something in his hand, from which another column of electric fire shot out again. I couldn't lift my head. I couldn't even keep my eyes open. Before my eyelids gave up, I saw Cub falling down next to me, smoke rising from his head.

18

The noxious smell of ammonia salt woke me up. My temples felt like a hammer was pounding them. The pain pulsated with my heart and was compounded by Baelz's voice. My head, arms, and legs were strapped to a chair. I couldn't move at all. I was in the same room as before. To my left, Cub was also strapped in another chair, but he was still out. His jacket had a hole burned through it. Wires ran from a machine to a headset; a woman seemed to be adjusting things on the machine's screen. She had brown features, faked pumped-up lips, and dark brown hair.

Baelz came up to me, holding a metallic shining device; it looked like a flame thrower with a canister attached to the handle, but the barrel was much bigger, like a large, elongated drum.

Baelz brought the device up to his lips and kissed it.

"You like my toy? I knew it could handle your boy. It knocked him right out. Though he is pretty tough. I thought it would vaporize the guy, but it only knocked him out. I know your boy has special skills. I had to take precautions." He stood in front of me. "This is my plasma gun. It works on the same principle as a flame thrower, but there are key differences. You will appreciate this. You see, this canister here has ionized gas which gets released when I squeeze the trigger. The gas goes through the chamber which has electromagnetic coils. These coils propel the gas into incredible heat, and out it goes. A blast of super-hot ionized plasma." He grabbed my face so as to make me look at him. "Pay attention. The drug should be wearing off by now. I knew you couldn't resist the drink. Haha."

"I'm going to carve you up the way I did Kirch," I managed to say, my voice slurred.

"How do you do it? I read up on you. How do you do your psychic thing? How did you fly into the sky like that? Did Spinoza give you a special way to connect to the parallel universe? Is that how you could defy gravity?"

"I'm going to enjoy hearing you scream."

"Give me the equation or I'll have to play with my toy. . . on you. And if you can survive my toy, we'll extract the equation from your brain. Lisa is very good with that. Aren't you, Lisa?" Baelz turned to the woman and squinted.

"You bet, darling. If it's in there, I'll find it."

"I'm going to cut up your shiny turtle head until you bleed to death."

"Okay. Here it goes."

Baelz pointed the plasma gun at my right hand. A burst of red-hot gas hit my hand. The hand literally evaporated, and smoke started to rise. Pain shot up my arm. A burnt stump remained, and there was no bleeding.

He clicked his tongue and said, "How are you going to cut me up now? You've got only one hand."

He was going for my left hand next. I had to do something before he burned it off, too. That would be the end of me; I could heal, but regrowing a limb was probably impossible. I looked down at the black flame and tried to wake it up. I channeled my pain into my left hand and pushed and pushed. The black flame rose. "Goddamn you!" I screamed at the black flame. "Wake up, wake up!"

Baelz stared at me with disbelief. "Your boy can't help you. He can't hear you. And I'll let you know a secret. I bought him. With a lot of money. That was why he retrieved Spinoza from Kirch. Do you think he would risk his life for you? I also gave him a tracker. That's how I found you. And the briefcase of money of course.

Always have redundancy. But I never trust a turncoat, so once I have you, I have to get rid of him too. And, I won't have to pay him."

I grunted, concentrated, and pushed the blood into my left hand.

Baelz aimed the plasma gun at my left hand and fired. The hot gas hit the black flame, which rose and got bigger as if it was feeding, though only I could see it.

"What the fuck!" Baelz screamed.

He shot the plasma gun again. The black flame got even bigger. And as the gas hit the black flame, it became visible.

"What the fuck is that?" he uttered. "What have you got on your hand?"

"Hahahaha! I'm going to cut you up good."

Baelz put the plasma gun closer to my hand and fired. The hot gas lit up the black flame, and Baelz fixed his eyes on it. A flick of the black flame, like a tongue, followed the gas right into the plasma gun's chamber. A loud pop boomed from inside the gun and it flew out of Baelz's hand, across the room, and hit the wall.

"What the fuck!" he screamed.

"I'm going cut. . ."

I felt a pain in my neck and turned toward it. Lisa had stuck a needle into my neck and was squeezing the syringe. I felt the drug flowing up into my head, warm and sedating. Immediately I became very drowsy, and I couldn't breathe. I tried my best to take deep breaths.

"You feel pretty good right? It's good stuff," she said to me. Her sharp eyes studied me, and her rouged, pumped-up lips smiled. "Josh, let me get it for you."

"Did you see it?" Baelz said. "The black thing on his hand? What tha fuck. It was sucking the plasma."

"Relax. Let me put the machine on him and be done with it."

"All right. Get on with it. I'm going to get another plasma gun. I'll see if I can burn that hand off too," Baelz said and went off. His shape became blurry as he exited the room.

She undid the strap around my head, put on the headset, and the machine began to buzz. She tapped on a keyboard, and my head started to burn with a thousand electric pinpricks.

"Spinoza, Spinoza, Spinoza," she said softly.

I couldn't help but think about Elliot and his face just before the black void took him.

"Elliot, Elliot, Elliot," she continued.

The night before, when we'd sat around the fire, had been really nice; it reminded me of high school days with Elliot and Margo.

"Hmm, you like that more. Of course. Elliot, Elliot. Equation. Equation," she seemed to whisper to me.

The notebook contained many equations, including the Void Equation. I could turn the pages in my mind one by one. She was right; whatever she had injected into me now made me high and drowsy. I raised my eyes toward the machine, and Lisa's eyes were fixed intently on the screen. She turned to me and smiled.

"I got it," she said.

"Got what?" I asked.

"The Void Equation. Isn't it much easier this way? I could never understand torture."

"What?"

"Here. Look," she said and turned the screen toward me.

I saw it, but I couldn't quite believe it. I had to look again. The device was literally reading my mind, capturing images from my visual cortex as I recalled them. I shook my head, but it was right there. On the screen were images of the notebook. The page was full of equations, and the next page was shown. The Void Equation was right there, one page interrupted by a blank page, just as I had seen it in the notebook.

"Arrrhhh!" I howled. That was why she had said Elliot's name. She had gotten me to remember the notebook, and she had taken the Void Equation right out of my mind.

Then, from the corner of my eye, I saw Cub twitch; his fingers moved, and his jaw jerked. I had to give Cub time to wake up, and I had to help him. I started to howl at the top of my lungs. "Arrrhhhh!"

"Easy, man. You're going to pop a vein," Lisa said.

My howl must have drawn Baelz, who marched in with another plasma gun.

"Keep it down. I don't like noise," Baelz said. "Show me what you've got."

"I got them all. All the equations, but how do you know which one is the Void Equation?" Lisa said. She unplugged a thumb drive from the machine and gave it to Baelz.

Baelz kissed the thumb drive and said, "Now I rule the world." He turned to me. "There is no secret anymore, buddy. I can take all your secrets. I know everything in that brain of yours. How do you like that? Hmmm?"

"I'll enjoy cutting you up. Arggghhhh," I howled.

All my anger came out; all the injustices of the world seemed concentrated through my voice box, and the black flame billowed from my left hand.

"Cut me up? I'll show you," Baelz growled. He aimed the plasma gun at Cub.

"Cub!" I screamed.

As if it were responding to my voice, the black flame zapped along the wires attached to my headset and dug into the mind-reading machine. Electricity crackled, and the machine burst into flame. Lisa let out a scream and ran out of the room.

"No! No!" Baelz yelled.

Cub opened his eyes. Smoke started to fill up the room.

"Cub, help!"

Cub took a couple of seconds and then he began to grunt, clenching his teeth and pulling at his arms. Veins popped out on his forehead and neck. The metal restraints over his arms burst.

Baelz's eyes bulged out as he squeezed the trigger. The hot plasma shot out and the black flame jumped at it; where they met, a silvery glow flickered.

"Motherfucker." Baelz pressed the plasma gun forward and put his weight into it. The silvery glow only brightened.

Cub ripped the strap off his head and then his legs. Seeing that, Baelz backed to the door and disappeared. Cub let me out.

"Good to have you back, Cub. Let's get out of here," I said. The smoke had thickened the air and made me cough.

"No, I'm going to cut him up. He took your hand," Cub said.

"We'll have our chance. Let's get out of here."

Cub picked up the chair and tossed it through the glass wall, which shattered.

"Let's go."

I went through the shattered glass. Outside, there was a stone ledge, beyond which was a straight drop of about fifty feet to the desert below. I held on with my left hand and took a few steps. Turning around, I saw that Cub was not there.

"Cub!" I called out.

A commotion was going on inside, and the air cracked and zapped as plasma guns shot off. There must have three or four guns going off, followed by Cub's scream. I turned back. I had to use the black flame to help Cub. Suddenly, the rest of the glass wall exploded. A plasma blast threw me off the ledge, and I fell straight down.

19

I fell headfirst. My arms reflexively straightened to break the fall, the black flame flared out, and, pop, I went into something. My face stopped inches above the ground. I got up, but my feet never touched the desert floor. It was as if I had fallen into an air bubble. I began to tumble through what seemed to be a transparent tunnel, which turned a corner here and there. My body, or what I felt was my body, sometimes moved like a flat piece of paper. Finally, I was thrown into an empty space. My first instinct was to look for Cub, but Baelz's compound and the rocky hills had vanished. All around me was the desert, stretching to the horizon; above me the sky was a dark blue with a subdued sun moving across it. A strange curvature of the air surrounded me, with my peripheral vision distorted and my central vision magnified. In the distance, cacti scattered far and wide, looking like stick men.

The sun was moving rather fast; it rose, passed over, and descended. The dark sky twinkled with stars, and then the sun rose again. And, though the sun passed above, I cast no shadow.

Except for my right hand, which was now a stump, my body was intact. The black flame on my left hand had disappeared. I looked down at the ground; my feet were floating above it, and no matter how hard I tried to stomp on the ground, my feet could not quite touch it. I started to run, I must have run for a mile, and my surroundings seemed to move past me only to remain exactly as they were when I had started. I jumped up and the ground moved up. I did this for a long time. At last I gave up. It was then that I realized I was not tired, nor was I breathing. I had no breath, no heartbeat.

I sat down and saw that I was actually hovering over the ground. I closed my eyes, but I could see everything through my eyelids.

A panic suddenly overcame me. Where was I? How was I to get out of here? I was certain that I could not travel any distance here, and even if I had managed to run a mile, I would never know, for there was no point of reference. I turned around and around, scanning the horizon for any clue of a difference in the surroundings, but the cacti all looked the same. Still, there was a phantasmagoric beauty in this place.

I needed to calm down. I sat still. Was this limbo? In this history of men, every myth had its kernel of truth. Perhaps this was limbo, which meant that someone had escaped it to spread the myth. If so, there must be a way out. Otherwise, limbo would not be limbo, but hell exemplified. Even if I wanted to kill myself, there was no way to do so.

The sun continued to pass overhead, interrupting the night. If one were really to think about it, everything belonged to darkness. The night had always been there. One could take away the sun, but never the night. Only the night could last forever. All this, a wise man had written about. I couldn't remember his name, though it made no difference now. Only the truth remained.

Since I got here, the sun had passed overhead three hundred and sixty-five times. Strangely, I could remember every one of its passages. I could have spent a year in limbo already, or only minutes. Time didn't make sense without its relation to space, and since space stayed the same, time ceased.

I lay down and stretched my legs, watching the sun passing over head, unchanging. It was not so bad; being here meant being without hunger or thirst. I could relive my life. I began to think about Cub, who was probably dead. He had betrayed me for money, but I couldn't blame him. There was no way he could have survived all those plasma guns. What about Elliot? Had he disappeared into nothingness forever or was he in limbo, too? Actually, being in limbo would be heaven for him. He could spend an eternity doing math.

The sun kept passing over head, totaling another year. I tried to silence my mind, but I could not. I began to mull over the past. My earliest memory came to me. I was lying in a crib, and my brother was trying to suffocate me by pinching my nose; my brother later died in a car accident when I was two years old. My first toy was a red car made of tin. Even now I could move it around, and the more I moved it around, the more I became that little boy. The boy went about his business, playing with his friends and having a toothache. One day, the boy saw a girl; her name was Brandy. The boy got violently sick from malaria. And after a fever dream, in which something in his brain exploded, he began to notice that he had a premonition for finding hidden things, and people, and sometimes he even saw things that were not there— the haloes of the dead. He continued to grow and adapted to his ability; during cards games he always won, and he always knew when something bad was about to happen. One day, he was old enough to go to high school, and he felt the happiness of spending time with Elliot and

Margo once more. Then came the time in the asylum, the notebook, cutting up Kirch, the battle, the appearance of the void and Elliot's death, and finally, the fall into the bubble.

This was what dying must feel like; when one has no future, one is forced to relive the past until the past becomes real. And with the outside unchanging, the eyes, even when they are wide open, will inevitably begin to see the only place where there is change, inside the mind. The past leads to the present, which will lead back to the past. An unbreakable loop.

I forced my mind not to think about my life, to cling instead onto nothing. I did this for a while, and it seemed to work. I was in the present of the bubble again. I raised my hands and was shocked to see the forelegs of a mantis. Turning my head every which way, I saw that I was a mantis. I hopped around the bubble, and the spines on my legs stuck to the bubble, allowing me to climb onto the top. What was happening? Suddenly, I fell heavily, and the air was knocked out of my lungs. I couldn't see the forelegs anymore; instead between my eyes was a long snout, that of a dolphin. I twisted and caught a glimpse of my flipper. Gathering all my strength, I beat the flipper against the ground and propped myself up; I stood for a moment and then flopped over. Instead of hitting the ground, I was almost weightless, flying. My wings flapped so fast that I could not see them; my lips had morphed into a long sharp beak, that of a hummingbird. I flew fast, aiming my sharp beak against the bubble, hoping to pop it. The moment it struck, I roared in pain. I shook my mane and backed away. Snorting loudly, I brought my paws up and saw that I was a lion. Then I changed again and again into forms of animals and even plants—a rose bush, an oak tree, a patch of moss; some of the animals and most of the plants I had never seen before. Finally, I was a man again, and I knew intuitively that I had been all those forms of life before.

Now I understood Elliot's message—Daniel, remember, beyond time. Somehow Elliot had also remembered all his previous existences.

After reliving all those life forms, I suddenly realized that I was not so much trapped inside the bubble but inside the mind itself. I couldn't get out of it. Another eighteen years passed, and with each year, I relived all my previous existences, resurrecting more and more meticulous details. The smell and touch became more vivid, and the pain and heartache become more wrenching. At last, each loop led to the present, which lasted a shorter and shorter time, before my mind jumped to the beginning again, and during this brief present I was able to have enough lucidity of mind to think. Soon, however, my mind drifted and there I was again, an insect.

Was there anything in the expanse of all my previous existences that could help me? I had relived each moment, even the long-forgotten moments that had only now been dug out from the hidden crevices. Nothing. There was no mystery in it, each moment understood and dissected to its ultimate motive. The sun passed over head with the equivalent of twenty years before it came to me.

The key was Elliot's equation. Its discovery had started the change in the world, and, thus, in me. It was the key to reality and to existence, I knew it now. The Void Equation would rip through space; it had shown me reality. How blind I had been. Perhaps it was why people like Kirch and Baelz had instinctively wanted it, not for its power, but something deep in them also knew that the Void Equation would show them reality.

My life now stopped with the notebook. I turned the pages until where half the equation had been written and then there was a blank page. Elliot had put the blank page there for a purpose. Now I knew he meant to separate the two halves of the equation. If the two halves were put together, the void would appear. That was what he had done during the battle, holding the two pieces of paper in his hand. Here was the mystery that I was looking for. I could spend an eternity trying to decipher the equation and each moment would differ from the next. I began to copy each symbol into the air, but nothing happened. I did this over and over, perhaps a hundred times. Could I have remembered the equation incorrectly? Then I changed one symbol in the equation. Then I rewrote the equation, changing another symbol. I must have done it a million times, trying a million variations, and remembering them all, until the air itself seemed to remember it, too, as if there was a consciousness witnessing me and goading me on. Finally, the air began to flicker. The symbols glowed. And there it was, the Void Equation written in the air.

A tiny dot, the blackest of black, the size of a needle's eye, opened from the middle of the equation. It started to suck in light; sunlight from above curved and vanished into the tiny hole. I stared at it.

Now I realized another thing, that the greatest gift a man has is the ability to end his life at will. I hesitated, but only for a moment. Then I put a finger into the hole, and it sucked me in.

20

did not die.

I opened my eyes to white light. The light was uniform and stretched to the infinite horizon. Up or down, I couldn't tell; I could not orient myself. I was floating. Reflexively, I looked at my hands. Slowly, I curled my legs and flexed my neck; now I could see my whole body. I was completely naked. My fingers ran over my skin, which was without scars. All the wounds I had suffered had vanished. The air flowed into my nostrils so sweetly. The temperature was perfect, neither cold nor warm. My heart beat inside my chest. I could see a million times more clearly. I had never felt better. In fact, I was me, more me than ever. Now I knew that this was real. Only by being here, only through this contrast could I see that the world that I had known all my life was utterly faked.

But something was not right. I brought my hands up close. They were both there; my right hand had regrown. Not only that they looked to be the hands of a young kid. What was happening to me? Twisting about, I examined myself more closely. My body was that of a child. I wished I could see my own face. But something was moving under my skin, like a minute wave rolling from head to toe. And with each wave, my body was getting bigger.

This went on for some time. Minutes or years, I knew not which. At last, it stopped because finally, I felt gravity. I was lying on a surface of the same ambient light. I got up and examined my body one more time; it looked about the same to me, the same as before I had tumbled into the bubble. I studied my surroundings. In all directions, there was the same white light. Was this another bubble of some sort? Another limbo, another hell? Would my mind soon revert back to the past again? But, something was different about this place; each breath I took felt real, more real than ever before. I stepped forward, and the light changed. The light illuminated a path for me, at the end of which I saw a grayish shade resembling a wall. I touched the wall and a portion of it vanished, opening up like a window, though there was nothing to separate the inside from the outside. On the outside, stars and galaxies twirled about. I stuck out my hand, and stars clung to my fingers as if they were a billion particles of sand. I moved along the wall, and the opening followed; the universe unfolded. "Hah," I uttered, mesmerized.

After moving along the wall for a while, I came to an end. Here a portal appeared. I put a hand forward, piercing what seemed to be a curtain of light or the surface of water. With a deep breath, I stepped forward.

As I went through, my body was now enclosed in an elastic white material, from neck to toes, which felt as though it was a second skin. The sight of the outside shocked me. Beyond the wall was a vast empty space, perhaps the size of the Grand Canyon. I was suspended in midair, upright. I looked up and down; rows and rows of exactly the same type of portals stacked one upon another, stretching into the distance, curving around to the other side where it was too far for me to see clearly. My leg moved one tentative step forward, and I started to glide through space, as if my thoughts alone could propel my body.

"Hello!" I hollered.

My voice faded into the distance; not even an echo returned. I glided along the rows of portals, sticking my head in one and then another at a distance. I did it a dozen times; they were all empty. I turned to the opposite side and glided toward it. It took a long time to cross, but finally I was there. Again, everything appeared exactly the same, as though I had stayed in place. I decided to go through a portal. Once inside, I went to a wall. The wall opened up as it did before; beyond was the universe, though it was different from before. I put my hands up, and the stars seemed to move, responding to my hands. I waved and beckoned; the stars came closer and closer. I kept at it until a star system came to view. I studied the planets; they were all dead, lifeless rocks. The sun caught my eyes. I pulled closer and closer to it. An atomic fire flowed across its surface. I felt its warmth on my face, and I pulled it even closer. It was getting hotter. A blast abruptly blew at my face, scorching it. I flung myself back, falling down. The back of my head hit the floor, and I slid through the portal. Outside, I stumbled uncontrollably, spinning fast.

I must have passed out. When I came to, my body jerked, shocked beyond belief. Before me was a man with long wavy brown hair, and a thick wavy beard hanging down to his chest. A golden twinkling halo radiated from him. He wore a long white robe, as if he had come straight from a Christmas catalog. He was floating over me. His deep eyes scrutinized me, seeming to see through me, everything about me, all the instances of my life all at once.

My mouth hung open. Everything inside me froze. In the depth of my mind, I knew who he was. Love and hate, hope and despair, erupted and churned inside me. All at once, I cried and laughed. I gazed at him for a long, long time.

"I am the Lord, your God."

21

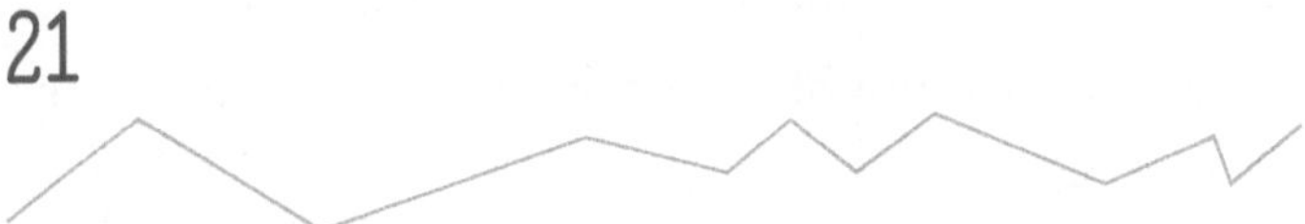

"**F**uck you."

I didn't know why I said that, and yet I knew exactly why. I didn't want to and yet wanted to scream it at the top of my lungs. It was as if all the injustices that had long plagued our species had now been vindicated, as if I were judge and executioner to the omnipotent as if it was not just I who had said it, but all the cells in my body, all the human beings alive and dead, all united in one voice.

"Fuck you," I said again.

And it felt good. Really good. These two are the most cathartic words ever invented. The second time came from me. It was personal. I should have felt a sense of sanctimonious dread, but I just didn't care anymore. Perhaps I had stayed in the asylum for too long.

"Justice?" God said, though, as before, his lips didn't move. I just heard his voice in my head, reverberating through every little nook of my brain.

Beyond my control, my body stood upright. I was now standing on the same ambient white light, and God hovered higher than me and looked down at me.

"I've always thought justice is better than love. Love is corruptible," God said.

I said nothing.

"I see your mind, all of your life. You're seeking justice." A holographic projection of my life appeared in the air, from the moment I was born speeding quickly to teenage years to adulthood; it spared nothing, not even the moment when I had first masturbated.

"You've been spying on me all my life?"

"No. I've only now examined your world, and hence your life. Ever since I received the signal and your arrival. Until now, your world has not been significant."

"My world?" I said.

"Yes, among trillions of others existing right now."

"That's why you presented yourself as God. The Hebrew God."

"Yes, if I were to come to your world, that role would most precisely describe me."

"Shouldn't you appear as a burning bush? Shouldn't you speak Hebrew?

"If I did, how would you understand? I command trillions of languages, all the languages of your species."

"So, the burning bush, the ten commandments, the Hebrew God, Jesus, all that was not from you."

"No."

"So, man was not made in God's image?"

"No, of course not. There are other species much more beautiful than you. Your species, as most species, survives by creating myths. Once a world is created, I never interfere."

So, God had no idea what was going on in his creation, his sick creation.

"You had no idea then what's going on in my world," I said.

"Not specifically your world, but countless similar worlds existed before and are existing now, some better, some worse. So yes, I do know. Hence your demand for justice."

Something in his voice just snapped me. Maybe it was the logical, matter-of-fact tone. I jumped up and punched him in the face. But my fist went through thin air, through a hole in his face; his face simply parted, like the Red Sea, and then came back together.

"Is violence your way of justice?"

"Yes," I said curtly. "There is so much of it in my world. It's time you knew a little about it. You created billions of people. They are all sentient, and they suffer. They're innocent." I thought of Gizelle Cumberland.

"Not all. You know that," God said. "You are made to be conscious, intelligent, and to have choice."

"I've heard it all before. It doesn't make it right," I said, shaking my head. "If only I could have your power, I would show you justice."

"So be it," God said.

Then he said nothing more. A moment later, a portal sped from the other side and stopped in front of me. The color of the portal changed, and I saw myself in it, as if the portal had become a mirror. Now I could see that my face was unblemished, the scars on my forehead had disappeared, and my white hair had turned to its natural black again. I turned to God, but something caught the corner of my eye, and I jerked back to the portal. My reflection hadn't moved at all. My heart jumped. It was not my reflection, but another me. He began to walk through the portal and approached me.

"Is this a joke?" I asked God.

"No. You said if you had my power, you would carry out justice. Since you can never have my power, I have reduced myself to you. He is identical to you in every way, down to the cells, the DNA, the knowledge, and the mind. Carry out your justice. Any pain you cause him, I will feel."

"Okay, we'll see how you like your medicine."

I paced around him. It was as if I was looking at myself in the mirror. It was a dirty trick because God must know that I couldn't possibly hurt someone who looked exactly like me. To do that I had to overcome the thought of hurting myself; it was a psychological barrier. When I had been trapped in the bubble, hadn't I thought that the ability to choose suicide was the greatest gift anyone could have? Now I had to use this power to choose. As I thought about this, I was getting angrier. I wasn't about to let God get away with it; I was going to hurt him even if I had to hurt myself first. Violence is the language of God.

"Are you ready?" I asked my doppelgänger.

"Yes. Ready when you're," my doppelgänger said.

I took a couple of steps across him as if I was still examining him. And bam, my right fist struck his jaw. He staggered back. I felt a pain my knuckles and knew that I had hurt him; I hoped God felt that. Now I put both my hands and started to dance around him. He did the same.

Not waiting for him to recover, I moved in fast and threw my right fist. He ducked back. I lunged forward with a left fist, which caught his left temple. His temple and jaw were becoming bruised. Pressing my advance to drop him, I moved in and threw a straight cut, aiming for his right eye, but he snapped to the left and his right hand clawed into my shoulder. A bunch of punches fell on my chest and face. I curled my arms around my face and jumped away.

"He's not me. He's God. He's God," I mumbled to myself.

My left fist hooked, and the right fist followed. He blocked left and right and pounded me right in the upper lip. My left fist jabbed back fast, hitting him in the cheek. Then I kicked his flank; he blocked, kneeled, and swung his leg. I fell. He stomped on me, but I caught his foot and twisted hard, and he, too, fell. We both jumped up and charged toward one another, punching ferociously at anything that we could punch. At times, we fell and rolled around very fast. We went back and forth for a long time. Finally, we were so exhausted and clinging onto each other, that I felt as if our minds merged and separated again because I thought I could feel his pain and he mine.

He knew all my moves, my reflexes, and he must also remember all the Krav Maga lessons I had taken. I had to disregard all the moves I knew, and I had to do something so unexpected that even I wouldn't anticipate. That was the only way to defeat him. Again, he rushed in close, held me by the neck, and snapped his head down over my nose. White twinkles filled my eyes, and blood flooded my mouth. Still rushing me backward, he tripped me and fell on top of me. He sat on my chest, and his fists rained down on my face. I couldn't see out of my right eye. "Ahhhhh!" I screamed, and with all my might, my legs pushed against the ground and flipped him off me. I barely got up when he charged me. My hands went into his hair and I leaped on him, wrapping my legs around his waist. He punched me in the stomach, in the chest, and tried to throw me off, but I wouldn't let go. Here I died, I decided. I pulled his face close to my face and put my mouth around his nose. I bit it off. It crunched between my teeth. Blood gushed out as he fell. And I punched him in the middle of his face, where his nose had been. Again, and again, and again. He lay still, bloodsoaked. My left eye gazed up at God, who watched me as I continued to pound and pound until my wrist felt as if it had been broken and my doppelgänger was motionless. I fell over, spat out the nose, and lay on my back looking straight up at God. Only now did I taste blood and feel the pain numbing my face and chest. I couldn't breathe.

"You sinned against us when you created us," I said, gasping for air, as I got up. "Now I kill you." I put my hands around his neck to choke him. I wanted his life to ebb away slowly. As I squeezed, the pain in my broken hand was incredible. Suddenly, he opened his eyes and gasped. His eyes were filled with terror. I wanted to stop, but I didn't. I put my weight into my hands and pressed down. Gargling noises came from his throat. Then he died.

22

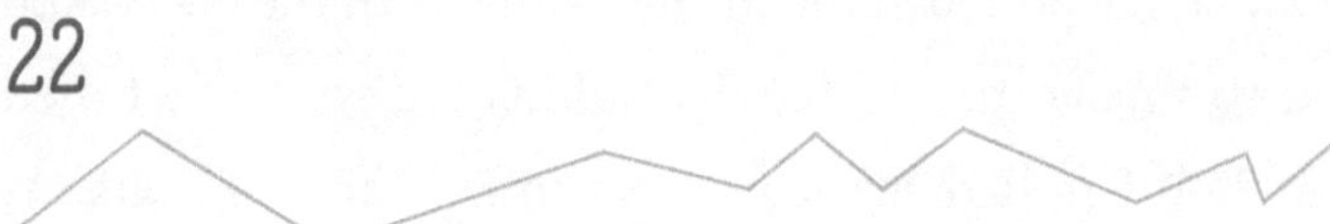

That was the day I killed God. That was how I did it. Of course, this is from my memory; I pieced the fight together much later when I sat down and wrote it all down. It had happened much too fast. I don't know if it had happened exactly like that, but I could be sure of two things, that I bit off his nose and that I choked him to death. I hoped he felt the pain. Though I couldn't say that I enjoyed it, or that I regretted it; it was simply as if a weight had been lifted off my being.

At last, when I let go of his neck, I kneeled next to him in the pool of blood, which was diffusing outward on the ambient white light. I began to cry uncontrollably; anger and sadness poured out of me. The body in front of me seemed like just another schmuck; it was I, and it was as if I hadn't killed God at all, only myself. I waited for God's wrath.

"Rise," God said.

Involuntarily, I felt myself standing up. The swelling and the pain in my face disappeared, my vision returned, and my hand returned to its former shape. I felt good again and could breathe easily. And my doppelgänger simply vaporized and vanished, merging with the floor, blood and all.

"What now?"

"You have rendered justice. Now you must have questions," God said. "And there is work to do."

"Was he real? How did he just vaporize like that?" I asked God.

"Yes, he was as real as you. It's similar to nanotechnology in your world. The strings can form anything, even living things, machine, inanimate objects. Hence your face can return as it was, and your hand."

"I am made of the same stuff here?"

"Yes. It allows us to be immortal. We never age, we never die. Our minds go on until the end of time."

"Where am I exactly?"

"My world."

Abruptly, we seemed to move up fast, seemingly floating through the air. The portals separated, and a long passage opened before us and came careening through us. Then I realized that we weren't moving at all, but our environment was moving instead, or some sort of visual representation of our environment was changing. A vista opened vast and awe-inspiring. It was a giant sphere the size of the moon; only a city covered the inner surface. I could only describe it as a city because I had no other word for it. There were structures made of light and dark matter, shifting constantly. The air buzzed with objects of all shapes moving about. Massive tentacles, resembling trees, linked these structures. Though at a distance, I saw creatures so distinct from one another that they must have belonged to different species; they all seemed to be doing different tasks. In the center of the sphere, a small star rotated; one side of it was as bright as the sun, but the other side was completely dark, thus giving the city a day and a night.

"I will explain to you using words that you can understand, though they may not describe the truth exactly. Your language is inadequate," God said. "Our universe is similar to your universe. We have stars and planets, and other astronomical phenomena. Our physical laws are similar to yours, with very small differences, which I will elaborate on. We are inside a ship. This is our city. That star is our clock. Though we have night, we have no need for sleep. Instead, we have moments of contemplation. Most of our time is devoted to finding solutions."

"Like Spinoza."

"Yes. If we were to say that your universe is comparable to this universe, then our ship is about a hundred times the size of your sun."

The view of the city morphed, cutting through what looked like the innards of the ship. There were moving parts too gigantic to comprehend. Lights and flows of energy crisscrossed in a bewildering configuration. At last, our point of view was from outside the ship. The ship was a black mass, indistinguishable from the black sky, and its size could only be realized by a star near the rear of the ship.

"We are seeing the ship from ten light minutes away."

"Is the ship taking in the star for energy?" I asked.

"No. Quite the opposite. The ship is giving birth to the star," God said.

"No," I gasped uncontrollably and gazed at God. Only now did I realize the extent of his power, which shook my very being. "You give birth to the star?"

"Yes."

"How long have you existed?"

"To use your time, I have been here about five billion years."

"So, you had a beginning?" I said excitedly. This would definitely alter my conception of God.

"Yes."

"Where did you come from?"

The view changed again. In front of us, a battlefield unfolded on a desert; there must have been millions of creatures lining up on opposing sides. The creatures must have come from an alien planet because I had never seen them before. They were bipeds, tall, muscular, and fearsome, and they wielded long shining swords. Twin antennae jostled on their heads. Most were on their feet, and some were riding enormous animals with a single horn, a cross between a horse and a rhinoceros. The opposing lines of fighters began charging, and blood began to flow. They looked all the same except for the leader; his antennae were tall and blood red.

"I was The Red Lord. Kraa the Red," God said.

"That was you," I uttered. "You were once just a living thing."

"I was, and in many ways I still am. I have been evolving for five billion years."

"How did you get to this ship?"

"Our planet was ten times the size of your Earth. It was rich in life and diverse. It was beautiful in every way. Our species had evolved on it for millions of years. Our antennae could emit high frequency waves, allowing us to communicate telepathically. Just like you and most other species, we were prone to wars. I was King of the Hinter Land. One day, I decided to stop wars for all time. I wanted to unite the planet. When that battle ended, I was the supreme ruler of the planet. Before me lay ten million dead. Instead of being triumphant, I wanted none of it. Something changed in me during the battle; the tuning of millions of antennae must have caused a rift in reality. I saw how false it was. A few days later, during the victory feast, I left and went deep into the desert, hoping to die. For many days I meditated without food or water. And then, when I was near death, the portal opened for me."

"Is it a trans-dimensional gateway of some sort?"

"No. I came from inside the ship," God said.

"How?"

"Like you, I came from a computer simulation."

"Hah." I was speechless, but it made perfect sense.

"To put it into terms you can understand, the simulation generators are nothing like your computers. They can rearrange matter and dial physical laws. They can vary the mass of protons, neutrino, or the vibration of the string. Each variation is an experiment. Just like your universe, mine was formed inside the ship. Like your universe, my universe was a simulation, an experiment. There have been countless simulations. Each universe sometimes yields one and sometimes multiple sentient species. Sometimes they discover one another across the vastness of space, sometimes to cooperate and sometimes to destroy."

God showed me the countless universes. Some were magnificent, and some were dead and lifeless from the beginning.

"I was the first to come. After I came here, I spent the first thousand years learning about the ship. Without the need to eat or sleep, I roamed about, learning everything. I was able to expand my mind. Since then, others have come."

"Who built the ship?"

"The Ohms. They were an ancient species. They had succeeded in every way possible. They had survived themselves, the death of their own star, the supernovas, the gamma burst, but at last they disappeared. We still don't know why. Traces of their minds still linger in the ship. They built this ship for one purpose. To give birth to stars."

"Why?"

"This universe is twenty billion years old. Just look at the sky," God said and showed me the sky outside.

"It's so dark."

"Yes. This universe is in its final freeze. The few stars you see were seeded by this ship. The Ohms knew billions of years ago that the end of the universe would come. They foresaw the end and thus they built this ship. The ship collects matter as it travels, and from that matter it feeds itself and gives births to stars. These stars are like lamp posts throughout the universe. The stars mark the entrances to the tunnels which allow the ship to jump through space. However, to use an expression from your world, we are building sandcastles. The universe's expansion is accelerating. Very soon, in about two hundred thousand years, we will not be able to see even the stars that the ship recently seeded. By then, the ship will stop. We'll stay at one place and consume the last matter. At last, we, too, will freeze."

"That's still a long time," I said.

"The blink of an eye."

"It doesn't matter to me. I never wanted to go on anyway."

"I sometimes think that there is no difference between those who live forever, and those who disappear forever. The Ohms created the ship, the simulation generator, and us. They left a pathway for us to escape the simulation and to have life. We owe them to carry on, to complete their work."

"To do what?"

"To escape from this universe or to reverse the freeze."

"To escape from this universe? Are you suggesting that this is also a simulation?"

"No. This is the real universe."

"How do you know that?"

"First, we can travel faster than the speed of light whereas in the simulation you cannot; if you are a projection of the simulation, you can never travel faster than the projection itself. Second, there is no quantum entanglement in this universe; quantum entanglement is possible in the simulation because everything in the simulation is linked to an external force, an external clock. So, Bergson was right, and Einstein was wrong. Lastly, we have an equation that unifies all the physical forces of nature; inside the simulation, you will never be able to find the unifying equation because you will always be missing that external force that gives rise to all matters. Godel was right. Inside your universe, nothing can ever be logically complete."

I was surprised that I understood all that. My body was made of strings, just like God, and thus my mind was more intelligent than ever. I remembered the science and the equations that I had read in articles about Elliot, only now I could understand.

"If the Ohms were so superior, what was the point of creating the simulation?"

"To find questions and thus answers. They came to realize that there is always a missing factor, that the sum is always greater than its parts, that there is always a ghost in the machine. We cannot ask the machines to calculate answers to questions that do not yet exist. If we have the questions, we can find the answers. By using the simulation, we seek questions as much as answers.

More importantly, we restore the ghost in the machine. And since the Ohms, we have been using the simulation to find a solution to our predicament. The simulation has brought countless new knowledge. There are trillions of simulations running right now. There are only three criteria for the simulation, that physical laws are nearly the same as this universe, and that the simulated universe must expand until it freezes. Then the simulation begins over again. None of them has yet to survive the freeze."

"What is the third?"

"That the simulation would stop once something new is found."

"That makes perfect sense. The Void Equation is that something new; that was why it created a void when Elliot put it together. It was the simulator's way of letting you know that something new had been created."

"Correct."

"What about all the things I saw? The energy flows that I could take and give to Cub."

"The simulation was changing because of Spinoza's discovery."

"But Elliot found it three years ago. Why does it take so long for you to see it?"

"Your time."

"What? How long has it been for you?"

"The simulation of your universe began seven days ago. To use your time so you can understand. Your species evolved within the last nine seconds."

"No." My jaw dropped. I stared at God.

"Time is relative. You have experienced years. Your experience is no less valid than mine. The simulation generator simply speeds up your universe billions of times."

"All those billions of simulations, there must have been quadrillions, if not more, sentient beings who lived and died and suffered. All for your cause."

"To exist is to expend energy. To take energy from somewhere. Life is an injustice. It's a form of injustice, an insolvable problem. Maybe the freeze of the universe is the most ultimate form of justice. One must pay back everything in the end."

"Why did I still have a memory of the previous life forms? When I was in the bubble, I transformed into a grasshopper, a lion, a dolphin."

"There is nothing new under the sun. What has been will be again," God said. "Once a living being dies, its form is reorganized in the simulator operating system and memory; thus, you have lived many thousands of forms and have been reorganized many thousands of times. You were able to access it. Your mind is an anomaly as much as Elliot Spinoza's. Thus, three years ago, when he asked you for a suggestion, you were able to lead him in the right direction."

I could stand here for a million years and wouldn't finish my questions, so I asked the most important one. "What happens to me now?"

"You go back."

"Back to the fake world? To the simulation?"

"Everything is real in its own way. You're real because we created you. There is always a connection between the creator and his creation."

"What for? You already have something new from Elliot. Besides, my world will last not another second with all the psychotic billionaires running around."

"The ship is at the edge of the universe. We don't know what's beyond. We've sent countless probes. Nothing has come back. We can only go there with our mind, our imagination, and mathematics. The equations will map the way for us. Once we have the full map, the ship will take the journey. It is perhaps to a parallel universe," God said. "Elliot Spinoza's equation has given us more clues about the way. You will go back and help him. Protect him. Guide him in the right direction. See what more he can come up with."

"Hah." I chuckled. "Despite all your power, you couldn't find what Elliot found. A small, insignificant simulation."

"The most beautiful thing in the universe is a paradox."

"Now what?"

"You found the way here. You have the right to stay as we all did. In time you will change. I was once as blood thirsty as you. I will put you back at the exact moment you left. And Elliot Spinoza where he disappeared. I will make you whole."

"If I choose to, can I switch with another person?" I asked. I thought of Elliot; he deserved to be here.

"Yes. It is your choice."

"I'm curious. How many sentient beings have escaped from each simulation?"

"One for every quadrillion simulations."

 I was speechless.

"I will need some help," I said at last.

"Yes."

"I will need the black flame."

"Very well. I will see you soon enough."

"Wait. One last thing. Did you feel the pain when I fought you?"

"Yes, I felt his and yours. It was as though I was back on my planet and in battle again."

I thought I saw a smile on God's face. "It's time I bring justice to my world," I said.

I began to fall through the floor of ambient white light.

23

I was back in the Nevada desert. I resumed my fall, headfirst, in the exact spot where I had been. My arms reflexively straightened to break the fall, and the black flame flared out. It dug into the ground and held me in the air, just inches from a sharp rock. It must be God's sense of humor to put me back on Earth as I was falling, but at least I had my right hand again. I looked to the rocky cliff of the hill, and the black flame clasped its sharp edge into it, like a claw, and propelled me up. The black flame was much darker, thicker, and just by thinking, it did what I wanted.

The air was still crackling from the plasma guns. From inside the room, blasts of hot plasma shot out into the desert air. I heard Cub's screams. I had to get in there. I came back through the shattered glass wall. Cub was hiding behind the mind-reading machine; its wires had melted, and the metal frame was red-hot. Baelz was standing behind three of his men and goading them on. His men were training their plasma guns on Cub.

"No way," Baelz said. Glistening sweat dotted his bald head; the fiendish excitement on his face turned to amazement as he saw me.

My left hand reached out; the black flame jumped to meet the plasma blasts in three prongs, like a three-headed snake, and absorbed the energy. The black flame glinted silver where it met the blasts. And then, as the men watched helplessly with wide eyes, three long spikes of the black flame reached inside the plasma guns, and Boom! the guns exploded out of their hands. Baelz turned and ran. The men grabbed their handguns and shot at me. I ducked, but the black flame split into a dozen sharp points, each cutting down the bullets in midair. "Urgg-ggghhh!" I growled, wanting to cut them up. And just like that, the sharp spikes of the black flame jabbed the men, like a sewing machine needle, at incredible speed. Before I could stop, they were three piles of meat collapsing on the floor. Blood drenched the entire room, and a foul fecal smell thickened the air; apparently their guts had been cut open as well.

"Back!" I shouted. The black flame withdrew back to my hand. I had to take a moment to squelch nausea rising from my stomach. I came to Cub. He was hurt; the sides of his arms were red and swollen from the heat. "Are you okay?"

"I'll manage," he said. "How did you do that? What's that thing on your hand?"

"I'll tell you later. Now we have to stop Baelz. He's got the equation."

"How?"

"He just took it out of my brain with that machine. We've got to stop him."

Cub picked up two handguns on the floor and wiped the blood off them. We headed out. This time, I was leading the way. I used the black flame like a shield. The next room was quite large, a living room of sorts. It had a billiard table, a full bar, chandeliers, dining tables, and an Andy Warhol on the wall. We raced through it and came to a bedroom. Everything in it was red, and it had the appearance of a dominatrix pad. The round bed had poles all around it, and a mirror on the ceiling. A table displayed all the sex paraphernalia—dildos, handcuffs, whips, masks, robes, knives, candles, stilettos, along with cocaine and pills. A faint smell of feces hung in the air.

"This guy is a sick bastard. Let's get him," I said.

Across the bedroom was a secret door, which was ajar. We went through it and down a staircase. Then there was a maze of hallways, turning left and right. A guard in a black uniform exited a door as we were racing down it. Before he could raise his automatic rifle, the black flame jumped at him and minced him up like hamburger meat. I couldn't get my eyes off it; I was developing a morbid fascination with this killing method. Maybe I should cut their heads off instead; it would be much cleaner. Cub picked up the rifle, and we ran down the hallway.

We burst through a door and halted abruptly. Beyond it was an enormous helicopter pad, which had been dug into the mountain. About twenty guards were standing around the pad, and they all snapped their weapons at us in unison. Three helicopters lined up neatly along the side, and another one was ready to take off. The roof was retracting, opening up to the sky above, and the helicopter was whipping up a strong draft. Baelz was standing by it; he turned, saw us, and got into the helicopter, which started to ascend, wobbling a little. The moment the helicopter cleared the roof, the guards fired. The black flame billowed into a giant umbrella, undulating like the surface of water, and, just as the bullets neared, a sharp spike rose and struck them down. Bullets littered the floor. Safe behind the black flame, Cub fired back, picking them off one by one. I counted five dead, and the rest started to retreat through a door on the other side.

"Let them go," I said. I looked over the helicopters. The two closest to us had bullets holes all over them.

The last one seemed to be intact and had only a couple of bullet holes in it. "Cub, let's get out of here. We have to get Elliot."

"What? He disappeared. The void took him. You saw it." Cub glared at me.

"I know, but God put him back there. The exact spot where he disappeared."

Cub just shook his head and went on. "Did God tell you this?"

"Yes, he did."

Cub's jaw dropped. "You talked to God?"

"Yes."

"Well, considering all the things that happened. . . okay. I can get us back there."

Just as Cub was about to hop in the helicopter, a nearby door popped open onto the helipad and Lisa ran out.

"I had to get my . . ." she started but stopped. Her eyes glared at us. She was wearing black Louboutin stilettos and a turquoise mini-skirt and holding a hand-bag. ". . . my. . . my handbag." She held it up for us to see. It was a red crocodile Hermes handbag. Her left hand was holding it by one strap so that it hung open. Very quickly, her right hand reached in and pulled out a Walther PPK gun. A shot buzzed my ear. My left hand flung out; the black flame shot out like a blade and went back. She stood motionless, and then her head rolled off her shoulders. Blood squirted from her neck. Then, she dropped to the floor.

"Oh," Cub murmured.

"Start it up, Cub. Let's go," I said. Despite what she had done to me, I would have given her safe passage to wherever she had wanted to go. I didn't feel the need to extract justice from her, though she deserved it. "She must have missed the ride with Baelz."

"Not good to be late. Sometimes you pay with your life," Cub said.

As the helicopter lifted, I surveyed the surroundings. I could never guess the true extent of the compound, which had been excavated into the rocky hill. From above, it was indistinguishable from the desert floor.

Except for the constant buzz of the engine, it was rather peaceful. Only now could I think about what I had been through. If I didn't have the black flame, I would have thought it had been an elaborate dream. This world now seemed fake; all the fights in this world now seemed to have the same importance as sand falling in the desert. The real fight was out there with God. The fight against eternal death.

"I'm sorry I betrayed you," Cub said at last.

"It's okay. You redeemed yourself just in time."

"He promised me so much money. I've never had that kind of money in my life."

"Don't worry about it. I would be tempted too. I would have done the same thing."

"No, you wouldn't. You're different."

"When this is done, I'll make sure you have all the money you need," I said. "I will sell the asylum and give it to you."

"Really? If you had all that money, why would you stay at the asylum?"

"It was the sanest place that I could find."

"Haha."

"When I ended up in the asylum, it was about to go bankrupt. All those people would have to be let go, some to other facilities, some to the streets. I couldn't let that happen. So, I bought the buildings and let the doctors operating it do so without rent. It's been profitable. The institute can survive on its own now. I will sell the buildings to them. I will give you the money. I owe you that much. Don't worry about the money. But for now, we'll get Elliot, and we'll go after Baelz before he does real damage with the Void Equation. And I can always go back to Vegas and win more."

We headed south. The sky was calm and sunny. To the west, I saw a highway; to the east, the desert stretched to the horizon. And I couldn't see any more of the energy columns shooting into space, or the haloes of flying dinosaurs. Soon Cub pointed to the crater where the missile had exploded and the big gouge in the earth that the void had caused. Then we saw a helicopter taking off from the near the crater.

"That's Baelz. He must have spotted Elliot from the satellite!" I yelled. "He took Elliot. Go after him."

Just then the engine started to sputter. I looked out and saw smoke.

"Probably from the gun fight," Cub said. "Hold on."

The rotor slowed and the helicopter suddenly dropped. We were falling. I flung the black flame out, and it encased the compartment. In a few seconds, we hit the ground and rolled. When we stopped, I pulled back the black flame. We got out and ran away from the wreckage, afraid that it might explode. The chassis of the helicopter was completely crushed; the blades and the tail had fallen off some distance away.

I looked up to the sky and cried, "Thank you, God!" The black flame had shielded us from the impact. We were shaken up but uninjured.

"You religious?" Cub said.

"It's not religion. It's science," I said. "C'mon."

We continued to walk. Though the sun was halfway to the horizon, the sunlight was still blinding. In the far distance, I thought I saw an overturned Humvee and some other vehicles.

"Do you see that?" I asked Cub, pointing.

He cupped his hands around his eyes, and after a moment, he said, "Yeah."

We picked up our pace.

Among the debris left over from the battle, only the dirt bikes were still working. All the trucks had been shot up, and those cut in half by the void had been hauled away by Baelz. He was probably trying to study them.

We found two bikes that were still usable and rode east, going slowly. Cub would jump over holes, and during stretches where the desert was smooth, he would ride at high speed, all the while hollering and cheering. I had never seen him happy like that. I followed behind him, cringing the whole time. After two hours, we reached the highway. We waved down a truck and gave them the bikes in return for a ride to Las Vegas.

In Las Vegas, we stayed away from the cameras and the hotels, even buying hats from a street vendor to hide our faces. Baelz's supercomputer, Lorrie, must be scanning for us, and Las Vegas must be one of their top targets. We couldn't rent a car or call an Uber without giving away our location, so we went around looking for buses. After asking around the parking lots of cheap hotels, we found a bus that was taking elderly tourists from Los Angeles; they were mainly Asian tourists—Filipinos, Chinese, and Vietnamese. The driver was keen on making money on the side, and he charged us fifty dollars each. The bus was scheduled to leave at 7 pm, and so we bought hotdogs from the street vendor. I asked to use the vendor's cellphone and called Ed Callow. He told me that there was no news with Margo and that she was still being held at FBI headquarters in Los Angeles. He also asked me if I could help finding the bodies of the victims of David Mageet, who was being held in the county jail, since the killer was a catatonic state and couldn't be interrogated. I told him I would help when I got back to LA, though I was intentionally vague about the timing. The call was probably being monitored.

After the call, we waited for the bus to leave. We stayed around the alley, avoiding the crowds and all the cameras snapping selfies. I realized that I could no longer see the ghost haloes from the past or the flows of energy. God must have reset the world.

At last, the bus crawled out of the parking lot with a busload of downcast elderly people, who had undoubtedly been hoodwinked out of their Social Security money. Stern resignation hung on their faces; they were probably telling themselves that they were in Vegas for fun, but I knew that they always had that hope of somehow winning it big and then giving it to their grandchildren and helping them in some way. Was there a profound injustice in their existence in God's plan?

We were relieved when the bus got to the I15 freeway heading south to Los Angeles. The two seats were far apart. Cub sat next to a friendly woman who was bent on feeding him.

"You eat. Good food," she said. Her wizened hand trembled as she handed him a Vietnamese sandwich.

Cub nodded and took it. Next, she gave him a pâté chaud, which he gulped down in one bite. Then she gave him bluish gelatinous dessert, which was followed by a bag of mango slices. She seemed to be saying something apologetic, as though she didn't mean to feed him out of sequence, when she whipped out a couple of hard-boiled eggs. Each time, Cub smiled, nodded, and ate. Finally, for the long trip ahead, she put a big bag of pork rinds between them to be eaten at their leisure.

Leaving the bright lights of Las Vegas behind, the bus went up the mountain pass. I thought ahead; once in Los Angeles, Cub and I would free Margo. I hoped I would be able to rip the white web off her head. After that, we would hunt down Baelz before he could use the Void Equation to do some real damage, free Elliot, and reunite him with Margo, fulfilling my vow to my friends. When we passed the checkpoint entering California, I closed my eyes. For the first time in days, I could sleep. I dreamed of the real world, of God's face, not the cartoonish man with the long golden beard, but the real face of Kraa the Red, in which there was such passion, and a true understanding of suffering. He had once been like me, a simulation; he had once killed and regretted and reached enlightenment, and so there was no need to ask him to understand. It was much better than asking a mythical God to understand me. He was a God I would willingly worship, knowing full well that he was neither infinite nor omnipotent, but only that he understood.

Suddenly, the bus stopped by the side of the road. I woke up. The jostling and whistling of the air brakes roused the passengers. The chattering of voices began. I saw the sign by the road: XYZ road. Then a police cruiser with its light flashing pulled over in front of the bus. Two cops got out with assault rifles. Behind us, there were many more police cruisers, and there were about a dozen cops surrounding the bus. Floodlights lit up the road. The bus driver opened the door, and a cop waved him out.

"This is California Highway Patrol. Everyone, please exit the bus," a voice commanded through a loudspeaker.

The passengers gasped; the people in the front got up and exited. Cub looked at me.

"Do nothing," I said. We only had two handguns, and I didn't want to hurt these innocent people. "Let's get off."

We exited the bus with our hands above our heads.

The cops swarmed around us with rifles.

They cuffed us and lead us to an empty field beside the road.

"You criminals?" the elderly lady, who had been feeding Cub, asked as we passed her.

Cub shook his head.

They marched us two hundred yards from the road and stopped.

"Where are you taking us?" Cub said mockingly. "Are you going to shoot us?"

"Don't worry, Cub. They won't hurt us," I said. "We are too valuable."

Once we were in the clearing, they stopped. They were communicating through their headsets, and a couple of minutes later, a helicopter descended. They put us in the back, which had been constructed to transport prisoners, a metal cage without door handles.They put chains through our handcuffs and shackled us to the floor. Then they put earmuffs on us, and the helicopter took off.

Soon we were flying over the low-lying cities outside Los Angeles.

Cub pulled off his earmuffs and motioned me to do the same.

"Let's get out," he screamed against the rotor noise.

"What do you mean?"

"I can break the cuffs. You shield us like the last crash," he said.

"No. It's too much risk. We'll wait. It's probably Baelz. It's better this way. We don't have to look for him."

We sat back and waited.

25

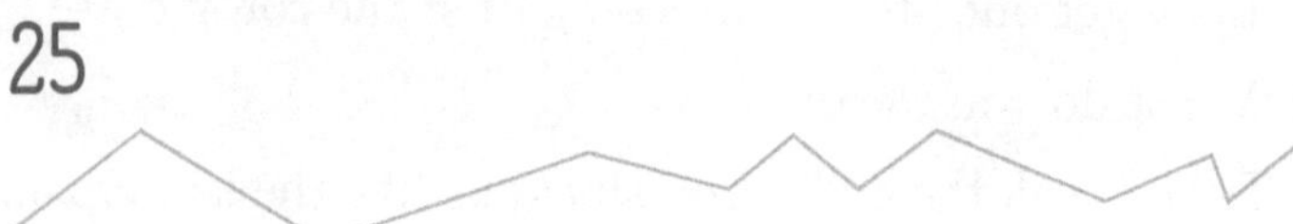

Finally, the helicopter landed on the rooftop of FBI building, the same one they had taken me to after I first left Margo at the hospital. We were met by armored guards with assault rifles and dark helmets. They led us out and promptly separated us.

"Don't worry. I'll get us out of here," I said as Cub was led away.

They took me down on an elevator, which descended for a long time. We were probably going underground. The elevator opened to a hallway, lit by fluorescent white lights mounted on the ceiling and lined by metal doors. They put me into an interrogation room, in which a metallic table and two chairs, were fixed to the floor. To one side was a one-way mirror. Each corner of the ceiling had a camera on it. On the table was a raised crossbar, and they cuffed me to it. Then they left.

I knew their game. They were going to make me wait. This was all part of their fear tactics. In a barren room with nothing but white fluorescent light and a cold metal table, the mind tended to wander, to feed itself fear, and to eventually to feed upon itself. Beyond one's control, one's stomach would begin to secrete gastric juices. An anxiousness tinged with pain would begin to rise from one's gut, until there was no gut remaining. One would, in fact, be turned into a spineless, gelatinous blob, waiting to gladly sign any confession and divulge all secrets. In here, behind each wall, stood a vast, faceless bureaucracy, designed to crush one's humanity until it disappeared completely. Minutes seemed like hours and hours months, a taste of what lay ahead if one were to resist.

They were waiting for me to be ready for them, but were they ready for me? I had been in the bubble in which the sun had passed overhead, year after year. In this room, I merely closed my eyes.

The door opened, and Jack Royce and Jonas Ortega entered. They were in their usual black suits, black ties, white shirt, and cocksure faces. Jonas took a seat at the table, and Jack leaned against the corner and crossed his arms. I had to chuckle; they were obviously playing good cop, bad cop.

"Do you know why you're here?" Ortega said.

"Are you the good cop?" I asked. I could see that my joking tone disturbed them. Without doubt they were expecting to see fear and meekness, just as I had shown them the first time they brought me in. The real reason why anyone would turn the other cheek is that his hands are too weak. Mine had the black flame, and I was ready to mince them into hamburger meat.

"You're being held for aiding and abetting terrorism. Your friend, Elliot Spinoza, is a terrorist. He has developed a weapon of mass destruction."

"Did Baelz tell you that?" I said as I watched him closely. If he was involved with Baelz, he showed no sign; he didn't even twitch.

"Baelz? Tell me about him."

"You're a foot soldier. Bring Conme here. I will tell him what he wants."

"You think the Deputy Director will waste time coming here for you?"

"He's already here. Tell him to come over," I said as I looked to the mirror. I was bluffing, but a slight movement of Ortega's eyes confirmed my suspicion.

"Look. . ."

"Shut the fuck up. Use your brain," I said, staring in his eyes. I had always liked using that phrase on the government bureaucrats. "Think about what I did to Kirch. You probably know already. How many did I kill in his compound? What I did to Baelz's men at his compound. How many did I kill? Why do you think I let you take me here? Tell Conme to come in here before I kill you all. Every single one in this building. And as for you two, I'll cut you up myself. That's a promise."

"Haha," Ortega chuckled.

I extended my left fingers, and the black flame flared out and extended like tentacles. Each tentacle curved around the handcuffs and the metal bar. I was directing the black flame and staring intently at it.

"You're scaring me. Hahaha," Ortega said.

Just then the door opened, and Jake Conme walked in.

"Out. Both of you," Conme commanded.

Royce and Ortega looked at each other and then at Conme.

"Now!" Conme yelled.

They left and closed the door.

"Here comes Baelz's dog," I said.

Conme leaned over the table and said, "The cameras are off. I can shoot you now and that's the end of it. Those guys in there are my guys. They will write the report anyway I want them to."

"Try it."

"This is your last chance. Who else has the Void Equation?"

"Is that what Baelz wants to know?"

"Your last chance."

"Take me to Margo. I know you have her here. Free my friends. We'll all walk out of here. If you don't, I'll kill all of you. And when you call in the Marine, the National Guards, the Air Force, hell, even the Navy, I'll bring the void. I'll rip up the earth apart if I have to. You must have seen the satellite feed."

"Haha. You've been staying in that asylum for too long. Who has the equation? Your last chance."

"Who decides? You or Baelz? Before he ran away, he told me you're his lap dog."

Conme became livid, and his hand flicked away his jacket and reached behind him. I raised my left hand, and the black flame cut the handcuff and the metal bar into small chunks. As he swung the gun around, I rose and threw the black flame, slicing the top of the gun off along with Conme's thumb. Blood squirted out. He screamed; his left hand grabbed his right hand to stem the bleeding. The door swung open; Royce and Ortega burst in, firing their handguns. The black flame swung to shield me, sliced down each bullet, and shot straight to their guns, cutting them in half. Then I thought of cutting their arrogant faces, not too deep, just below the skin; they deserved no less than a thousand cuts, each only a few millimeters. As soon as I thought this, they screamed and staggered out of the room with their hands clinging to their faces, blood dripping all over their suits. The black flame had carried out my thought instantly.

"I can't see," Royce screamed.

They both felt the wall as they tried to get away.

An alarm shrieked deafeningly. I heard footsteps down the hallway. I peeked out and saw men in black body armor and helmets, holding shields and assault rifles—a SWAT team. Behind them were many more men in black suits. Two men moved forward and led Royce and Ortega away.

"Get out," I told Conme. "I'm going to kill you last. You will bear witness to the death of all these men. Every single one of them in this building."

I pushed Conme out.

"Stand down!" he cried out. "Everyone, stand down."

I followed behind Conme.

"Tell them to bring my friend," I said.

"Bring him!" Conme hollered.

They opened the door down the hallway. As soon as one door opened, Cub came out. He came to me.

"See. Told you I could break the cuffs," he said, smiling. He was still wearing his handcuffs, but the chain was broken.

"Take us to Margaret Spinoza," I told Conme.

Still squeezing his right hand and groaning, he shuffled forward, dripping blood on the floor.

"Stand down. Go back to your posts!" Conme yelled.

The SWAT team backed away. We went down the hallway and then made several turns. Finally, Conme stopped in front of a door. He had to lean against the wall and breathed heavily, pale from blood loss and pain. It was a medical ward. There was a nursing station, and beyond were the patient rooms. A nurse saw Conme and came to his aid.

"Where is Margaret Spinoza?" I asked her.

Looking fearful, she pointed.

"Stay here and keep an eye on him," I told Cub.

I ran to the room. Margo had her eyes closed and was breathing on her own. She no longer had the intubation tube. There was an IV line snaking into her arm and electrodes were all over her body. The monitors chirped, beeped, and showed the tracing of her heart.

"Margo. Margo!" I called out. I took her hand. "Margo. I'm here."

I could see the white web shrouding her head; it was almost transparent, like a fine spiderweb. Her face fuzzed statically, now and then.

"Margo, wake up. Wake up. It's Daniel. I'm here."

The black flame crawled along her neck like moving water over her face, and into her hair, and as it did so, it seared the spiderweb and cast it away.

Suddenly, Margo took a deep breath and opened her eyes.

"Margo," I said.

She sat and looked at me.

"What happened to me? Where am I?" she asked.

"You just passed out. You're in the hospital, sort of. How do you feel?"

"I feel fine," she said and got out of bed as though nothing had happened. She had been changed into a hospital gown.

"I'll explain everything later, but we need to leave."

I went out and got a nurse to bring Margo her clothes and to remove the IV lines. At the nurse's station, Conme appeared calm after the nurse bandaged his hand.

"Let's go," I said, and then I turned to Conme, keeping my voice down so that only he could hear me. "If anyone tries anything, I'll take off your ears, then your arms. If they try a third time, I will go after everyone in this building. Room to room. Do you understand?"

He nodded.

To show him I meant what I said, I looked at the metal double door and waved my left hand. The black flame whirled around it, cutting a large circle, as if the metal just disappeared by itself. I stepped up and kicked in the middle of the circle, which flew out into the hallway and landed with a bang.

"Let's go," I said.

Cub pushed him out.

"Stand down!" Conme called out.

We made our way to an elevator and took it to the lobby. There were guards and a SWAT team in armor waiting for us. Again, Conme screamed at them to stand down. At last, we exited the front door. Cub held on to Conme until we cleared the building and were on the street.

"If you don't leave us alone, I'll find you. I'll kill you and everything you care about," I told Conme before I let him go. "I'll bring the void if I have to. I'll fuckin' split the earth in half if I have to. You don't believe me? Wait until tomorrow and see what I'll do to Baelz. His money won't protect him. Tell him I'm coming." From the moment they tracked us to the bus, I knew that we could never evade them for long. In this world of countless cameras, artificial intelligence, and facial recognition, they could always find us. They would only leave us alone if they believed that we would kill them all. And I would make Baelz an example. "Like I said. You can bring the Marines, the Air Force, and the Navy. I'll kill you all."

He simply stared at me without saying anything. I saw fear in his eyes, but also hatred. People like him don't back down reasonably. They do so because they have to.

26

We walked away and waited for a ride a block away; Margo still had her cell phone, so she called a Lyft.

"What is happening?" Margo asked me finally.

"When this has all passed, I'll explain everything to you."

She sighed but didn't press me.

Because the void had wrecked her house and the FBI had quarantined it, Margo wanted to go to a hotel.

"You have to disappear for now," I told her. "Baelz has Elliot and the Void Equation. Jake Conme wanted to know who else knows about it. Conme works for Baelz. You're not safe. Baelz will want to get rid of you and Elliot so that only he has the equation."

"Yes, I'll stop by the house to get the car. I'll leave town tonight," Margo said. "Promise you will bring Elliot to me."

"Yes," I said. I would bring her Elliot as soon as I could kill Baelz.

"It's not because I love Elliot more," she said hesitantly. "It's because I thought you could always take care of yourself."

Then we said nothing more. It was nearly two in the morning, and a cool mist was descending on us. In the deserted street, nostalgia also descended upon me. I felt as if we were back in high school. During high school, we had hung out late many times, often going out to see a movie, and after each movie we had gone to get a hamburger. Sometimes, we had gone to the beach and sneaked out onto the sand at midnight, lying there and looking up at the stars. We had been inseparable.

We took Lyft, and Margo got off at her house to get her car. She hugged me and gave me a kiss. I watched until she drove off. Then, Cub and I went to the asylum.

We got there at the darkest hour of the night. Everything stood motionless under the streetlights—the cars, the sidewalks, the maple trees, and even the moribund light itself. Suddenly, I missed all of this—the little concrete sign in front of the gate, the buildings with bars on the windows, the enormous yard beyond, where countless maples trees shed their leaves each autumn. I knew I would never see it again. I must have stood there a long time, just taking it in for the last time when I heard Cub.

"Are we going in?"

"No. We are just taking the car," I said.

The old Chevy was parked in the street in front of the asylum. I had hidden the key in a magnetic key holder under the car. I had a couple of cellphones in the car, and I texted Ed Callow that I would see him in the morning. We had to wait until the morning, so we slept a couple of hours in the car. Then I drove to Norms Restaurant, which was open twenty-four hours a day. There were a couple of early birds there, who were drinking coffee and reading from their phones. We sat in a booth and ordered pancakes, sausages, and eggs and toast.

"So, what do we do now?" Cub asked.

"I'll have to help Ed Callow with one thing before we get Baelz."

"Who?"

"A friend. A cop that I've been working with. We were working on a murder case. I've been helping him with some of the cold cases."

"Where is Baelz?"

"Here in LA. In his compound," I said, but I didn't know for sure. I couldn't sense anything.

It was a delicious breakfast, and after we had finished the last morsel, we drank coffee until around eight o'clock. Then, we drove to the county jail, where David Mageet, the child serial killer, was being held. I left Cub in the car.

Ed Callow was expecting me. He met me in the front and walked me in. It was a rundown minimum-security jail in East LA. The main building was a colossal structure leftover from the fifties; the tan paint was cracked and had faded. On the windows, the metal bars had rusted.

"Did you find Elliot Spinoza?" Ed asked.

"Yes, I did," I said, observing him.

"That's great. So, everything is settled?"

"Yes. I squared it up with Conme."

"Really? That doesn't sound like the FBI. They don't let you out so easily. Are they holding the Spinozas?"

"No. We gave them what they want," I lied

"Great."

Ed signed in, checked his weapon, a magnum revolver, and led me down the hallway. We went to a door marked Psychiatric Holding. Ed waved to a camera overhead, and they buzzed the door, behind which was another hallway lined with rooms. Each room had a small glass aperture through which we could see inside.

"I don't know what you can do, but I don't have any other option. The doc has seen this guy a dozen times. They forced a bunch of drugs down his throat, but he was still catatonic," Ed said. "We found him just like you said. Just sitting there on the side of the road, mumbling some stuff to himself over and over. Now he just sits there and stares straight ahead. He'll eat and drink, but he won't say a word."

"Okay, I'll see what I can do."

In front of the room, I stopped Ed from coming in with me.

"Give me ten minutes. I'll see if I can get him to talk," I told Ed.

"Okay. I'll be outside. Call if you need me."

The room was sparse; it had a bed and a bathroom. A faint stench hung in the air. David Mageet was sitting on the bed, staring straight ahead. The little black flame, which I had put on his head, started to move when I entered the room. His eyes went from side to side; he seemed to see it and followed it with his eyes. I put out my left hand. The little flame jumped from his head to my hand. Instantly Mageet jerked awake and seemed as if he didn't know where he was. Startled, he looked around the room.

"Where am I?" he said.

"Do you remember me?"

He stared at me. "You."

"Tell me where you buried the bodies. All six girls that you killed."

"You," he growled. "What did you do to me?"

"Tell me where you buried them. Otherwise I'll put you away again," I said. I held up my left hand. The black flame undulated like water.

He seemed to see it. His face tensed, crazed and sinister. He clenched his teeth, looking to the door, to the bathroom. His hands groped one another as though he didn't know what to do with them.

"There is no way out. You're in jail," I said.

Suddenly he jumped at me; his hands went for my neck. I couldn't kill him, not in here. I wanted what was in his mind. At the thought, the black flame shot out a long thin needle into his head. He froze. I wriggled out of his choke hold and pushed him down on the bed. Then I saw images in the black flame as if it was retrieving them from Mageet's memory. He was in church, singing hymns. He was cleaning and doing chores after the Sunday sermon, staying late. And when the night came, he carried a little girl's body from his trunk into the church's cemetery. He dug a deep hole and put the body in. I moved my finger back and forward, winding and rewinding through his memory; they were all there, the woods, the desert, the mountain, all the places where he had buried them. I saw, too, how he had watched them, snatched them, and raped them. Angry and disgusted, I looked at every nook in his brain, and finally, when I could no longer bear it, I pushed him away. But he wouldn't move. Where the black flame had entered his brain, a trickle of blood came out. His eyes stared without motion. I had unintentionally given him a lobotomy.

I left him in the room. He was no worse off than before. No one would know the difference. Outside, Ed had heard us.

"So, you got him to talk?" Ed said.

"Yeah. I got the locations for you."

I wrote down the details of where he could find the bodies.

"Where did you park?" Ed said and walked me out.

"Down the street."

As he walked with me, I felt a sense of unease, not in a psychic sense but observing Ed's demeanors. Even now, after knowing the truth about this world, I still could not escape its drama. Somehow, I couldn't help rectifying these injustices, for they were as real to me as the real world out there.

"Thanks. You really helped me," Ed said.

"Thanks for everything, Ed," I said, knowing that I would never see him again. I turned to him and shook his hand. "Take care of yourself."

"You do the same," Ed said.

The car was half a block away. I headed toward it.

Boom! Boom!

Two shots rang out and the bullets flew away from my chest. I looked down at my shirt; it had two holes in it, but there was no blood. I turned around. Ed was pointing his magnum at me. A whiff of smoke was still rising from the barrel. I ripped open my shirt to see if I was hurt. There was no blemish on the skin.

Boom! The gun fired another shot. My chest parted, and the bullet flew through the hole, just as God's face had parted when I had tried to hit him.

My eyes rose to Ed; there was a look of puzzlement and fear on his face.

"How?" Ed uttered.

"Oh, Ed. Not you too."

"Baelz. He. . ." he said but stopped and smiled wryly as if he was expecting and was ready for punishment.

He didn't have to say the rest. I understood that Baelz had bought him off with a lot of money the same way he had bought off Cub. I tried not to think bad thoughts or how to hurt Ed, because I knew the black flame would execute my thoughts instantly. Instead, I thought of our friendship; he had been my only friend for the past three years; he was my only connection to the world outside the asylum. Perhaps the escape from blood thirsty violence begins first with peaceful thoughts.

Cub had heard the gun shots and ran up behind me. He saw Ed's gun and was about to jump on Ed, but I held him back.

"Ed, go home," I said sadly.

In this world, the power of money was absolute, until now. When God put me back in the simulation, he had given my body all the qualities of a body in the real world; it must have been just the addition of a few lines of code. Now I had the power to take down the richest man in the world. But I longed for the real world, where money no longer existed.

27

The hunt for Baelz began. We went around the city in a great circle, and as Cub drove, I checked the sky. I couldn't see anything. There was no visual disturbance, no change in the color of the sky. All I had was a guess that he was in the city, but in the vastness of Los Angeles that meant nothing. He had many properties in Los Angeles, but which one? So, we continued in great circles around the city; eventually I homed in on Beverly Hills because Baelz had brought a mansion there recently.

Cub cruised along Hollywood Boulevard. He didn't seem too concerned with our mission; he looked relaxed and happy, watching the tourists teeming along the sidewalks, and the varied and colorful storefronts. After all this, I wished Cub would return to a normal life, to have the things that would bring him happiness—a wife, a child, a family.

Soon it was lunch time, so we went to one of those famous Hollywood delis and got pastrami sandwiches and vanilla milk shakes. It was as good as ever. The world was once more solid and consistent. And I had no clue where Baelz was. What Baelz could do with the Void Equation was limitless; he was profanely rich already, and now he could use the equation to become ruler of the world.

"Damn it," I said.

"What's wrong?" Cub asked as he sucked on the milk shake.

"I don't know where he is. I can't track him. I can sense that he's here, but I can't pinpoint his location."

"Look for him on the internet? You can find anyone on there."

"What a ridiculous idea. We need to find him by tonight." Why, why did I lose my psychic abilities, I asked myself?

Despite what I'd said to Cub, searching on the internet was actually the most logical solution. Using my cellphone, I began to search. I read through dozens of articles about Baelz, about all the properties he had amassed in New York and Los Angeles, about his business monopoly destroying all the small businesses in the world, and about his political power and connection to the money printer. I had to endure all the tabloid articles about his divorce settlement, and the woman he had cheated with. It turned out that woman was Lisa, the one I had beheaded. After an hour, I was exhausted from reading on the small screen and gave up. I fumed silently; in my mind, I imagined I could assess all the cameras in Los Angeles. They were connected to the internet, if only I knew how to hack into them. As I thought this, the black flame spread out like threads, wriggling into the cellphone. Then I saw it in my mind; I saw the street through the camera outside the deli. The view raced along the street, jumping from one camera to the next, heading to Beverly Hills, then from one estate to the next. At last there it was, I recognized the helicopter on the golf course. It was the same one in which Baelz had escaped from his Nevada compound.

"I got him," I said to Cub.

"Told you. You can find anyone on the internet."

Of course, it made sense to me that the black flame could access the mind of the serial killer David Mageet, as well as the internet; they were just different forms of the organization of matter. The black flame could get behind them and into them. It seemed as if there was nothing on Earth that the black flame could not penetrate, as if it was the key to this simulation. I had forgotten to ask God about the black flame, and I reminded myself I would ask about it when I returned to the real world.

Through the cameras of Baelz's estate, I looked around the compound and mapped it out. It was an enormous compound with a golf course and tall hedges all around the perimeter. There were a main house and then a couple smaller ones. Inside the main house, I saw the bald turtle head running around with a lot of men dressed in black uniforms. From their demeanor, they must be working on something important. Then they went into a room where there was no camera. They must be preparing to use the Void Equation somehow. Outside, several women were sunbathing by the pool. Guards were patrolling the golf courses with dogs.

We had to wait for nightfall. Suddenly, I remembered something.

"You don't have to do this, Cub," I said.

"I can do it."

"I'm sorry, Cub. I can't give you the energy anymore. I haven't seen any of it around."

"I don't need it. I still feel strong. I broke the handcuffs."

"Hmmm. That's good. Okay, if you're up to it," I wondered if God had given him permanent strength. "What about your injuries."

"They healed up. I'm fine."

Cub and I relaxed, ate dinner, and slept in the car. When it was about two in the morning, we headed to

Baelz's compound. At this hour, I figured most of the guards would be sleeping, and I wouldn't have to kill so many of them. Cub drove around the compound once and then parked in the street. We had no weapons except for two knives that Cub had found in the trunk.

"We have to get over the hedges. We'll go for the main house. He's in the main house. There are guards with dogs walking the grounds."

"Let's do this."

Knock, knock. The knock on the window startled me. A security guard in a black uniform had sneaked up next to the car, and after knocking, he stepped back and raised his hands. I rolled down the window, expecting him to tell us to move along, or that we weren't allowed to park there.

"Mr. Baelz would like to see you," he said.

"Okay," I said.

"Please drive to the front gate."

Cub drove to the front gate, which was already open for us, and up the driveway.

"I wonder what Baelz is planning. He's a sneaky bastard. Just one look at his face, you'll know right away."

"Easier this way."

About a dozen guards, all in black uniforms, were aiming their rifles at us. They led us into the main house. Through the front door was a stately reception area. From the high ceiling, a gigantic chandelier hung, its lights twinkling. There were original paintings on the walls, but the room had been emptied of the furniture, except for a Steinway grand piano. The entire floor had otherwise been cleared, and black tape marked the length of the floor.

Baelz was on the other side, standing behind several guards. He said, "Hey, we meet again. My satellite saw you guys circling around. So, I thought why not asked you to come in."

"Thanks. I'll enjoy cutting you up," I said and looked around at the guards. "Anyone here who doesn't want to die for this asshole should get out of here now."

Nobody budged. They must not have seen what we did to the guards in the Nevada compound, which was too bad. I noticed also that there was no one behind us. Just then, Baelz held up two pieces of paper.

"Hahaha. Got you. Here is the Void Equation. Do you think you're fast enough to run?" he said, smiling.

So that was why he had put the black tape on the floor. The earth was rotating toward him, and so if he were to put the void Equation together, the Void would take us. There was no way we could escape.

In a flash, Cub threw his knife at Baelz. The knife went high and barely scraped his shoulder. They opened fire on us. The black flame jumped out and shielded us; bullets clang as they fell to the floor.

"Hold your fire," Baelz screamed. "Hold your fire."

Then it was eerily quiet.

"I'm going to enjoy this. I want you to know that I don't give a shit about the extra dimension, the parallel universe. With this I'm going to rule this world. I want you to know that I'll cut Spinoza up the way you want to cut me up. How is that?"

I took the knife from my pocket.

"Here goes," Baelz said.

With a deliberate and ceremonious gesture, Baelz held up the two pieces of paper, just as Elliot had done. He put them together. Cub and I dove to the ground. But nothing happened.

Baelz's eyes bulged at the pieces of paper. He brought them slowly together, carefully lining them up. Still nothing.

Cub and I got up. Had God reset the simulation? First, I couldn't see the energy flows, and now the Void Equation didn't work.

"Hahaha," I laughed. Whatever the reason, it no longer worked.

"No, no, no, no!" Baelz screamed. "Kill them." Baelz backed out and disappeared.

Bullets rained down on us. The black flame flared out like a gigantic umbrella. The noise was deafening. I didn't want to kill any of them, just Baelz, but I needed to make a few examples. From the umbrella, the black flame flicked out like a long sword and cut off the head of the guard nearest to me. Blood squirted from the neck over the white marble floor. The others kept on firing. Then, the flame cut off another head. Blood sprayed out. But the smell of the blood seemed only to drive them crazier. Then I heard the strings of the piano breaking behind me, and I saw, from the corner of my eye, Cub picking it up and throwing it. Bullets riddled the piano as the guards scattered. The piano landed and broke, sending shards flying. Cub ran to a headless man, grabbed his rifle, and started shooting; he killed two men. Others retreated, and Cub followed them to the east wing. I headed after Baelz, to the west.

The house was a maze, with long hallways, and stairs. I went up the stairs, thinking that he might have gone to the roof. Perhaps a helicopter was waiting there. I found no one. I headed down and toward the back of the house.

A long hallway led to another room in the distance. I heard a commotion behind the doors along the hallway.

"I'll kill anyone who shoots at me," I hollered.

As I entered the room, I saw Elliot. Baelz was standing behind him and was pointing a plasma gun at his back. Several other men were pointing guns at me, but only two of them had plasma guns.

"Surprise, surprise," Baelz said.

"Are you okay?" I said to Elliot.

"I'm fine," Elliot said. He had the same carefree jovial look as always.

"You do anything, I fry him . . . crispy," Baelz said. "Get on your knees."

I dropped to my knees.

"Tell me why the Void Equation doesn't work, or I'll fry you," Baelz spoke to Elliot.

"He doesn't know," I said. "I don't know either."

"If I have to ask again, I'll fry his ear off."

"Okay. Okay. The system has been reset."

"What system? You're trying to fuck with me."

"None of this is real," I said.

"What do you mean?"

I saw that Elliot was taking something out of his pocket and shook my head, telling him not to.

"We are in a simulation."

"How do you know that?"

"Think about what you've witnessed. I can stop bullets. A void appeared out of an equation. How do you explain that? We are inside a simulation."

"Like a computer simulation."

"Yeah, but much more complex."

Elliot stared up at the ceiling as if he was calculating something.

"Why?"

"Because God wants us to ask questions and find answers."

"God? You're out of your mind."

"I call him God because for all intents and purposes he is God."

"You've met him?" Baelz asked, shaking his head.

"Yeah."

"I want to meet him, too," Baelz growled.

"Never your kind."

"No, it can't be. I'll figure it out," Baelz muttered. He backed toward the exit, dragging Elliot with him. Except for the two holding plasma guns, the rest of the guards backed away with him. "You follow us, I fry him. This is my new and improved plasma gun. Don't fuck with me." He turned to the two guards remaining. "Blast him if he moves."

I watched him intensely for a chance to act. As he backed away farther, he looked behind him. That was my chance. I raised my left hand and the black flame shot out, but a blast from a guard's plasma gun met it. The other guard also opened his plasma gun on me. The black flame turned silver. Baelz was nearing the door. He was getting away.

Suddenly, Elliot turned around and put his hands together. The void appeared. I saw Baelz's eyes bulge wide just before the void flew out, taking Baelz, the whole wall and all the guards with it, disappearing into the night sky.

A guard's arm dropped on the floor. The void had cut through his arm and taken his body.

The rest of the guards turned around to look, dropped their weapons, and ran away.

"Did you see that?" Elliot said excitedly.

"Yeah. But why didn't it work for Baelz? His machine had read my mind. He had a picture of the notebook and the equation. He couldn't make it work earlier."

"The equation in the notebook was wrong. I switched a couple of symbols," Elliot said, smiling. "We showed him. I knew he couldn't figure it out. There are only a couple of people in the world who can tell, and it would probably take them more than a few days. Haha."

That was why I had had to try a million times before I got it right, when I had been the bubble.

Just then I saw Cub; he had gone from the East Wing and circled around back. He called to us from the outside.

"Guys. We have to go. I hear sirens."

We all ran to the front of the house and got into my Chevy. Cub sped through the gate; along the street, we passed several fire trucks. We saw that the void had taken a wide swath of the neighborhood. Later, the newspaper would report that an unexplained event had taken five consecutive mansions and their owners, five billionaires.

Of that night, I would never forget Baelz's eyes just before the void took him; they were full of incredulity and horror.

28

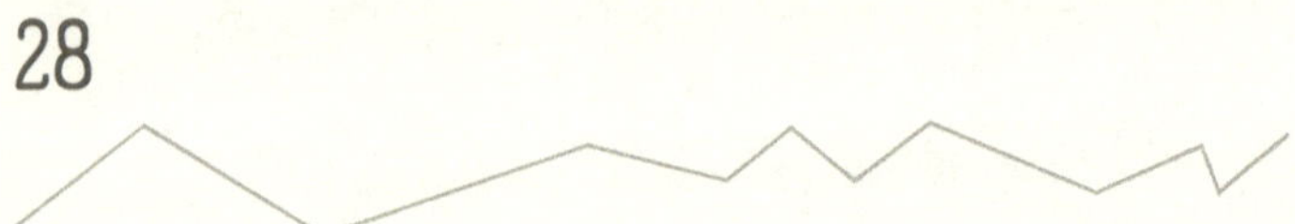

There are invisible things in the world, things that can never be measured or seen but only intuited. The Ohms knew this; that was why they created the simulation, to capture the unseen, to find things they themselves could not find. In a way, we are the manifestation of the difference which makes the sum greater than its parts.

They sinned against us the moment they created us, and for that the compensation was consciousness, so that we could know the sin against us but could also rise above nothingness, even just for a moment. There seemed to be no purpose to our existence, and paradoxically each of our existences had its precise purpose. We are the darkness against which light could shine.

For the months after I split from Cub, Elliot, and Margo, this was all I could think about. I hoped God could find a way to escape the deep freeze, but, if not, it would be a marvel to witness the end of the universe.

I made good on my promise to Cub; I gave Cub most of the money from the sale of the asylum. I said goodbye to cockatoo, nightingale, and sparrow. Then I hid out in Los Angeles, drifting from place to place. I used the black flame to surf the internet, to keep tabs on Jake Conme and anyone else still trying to get to Elliot. The best way to keep Elliot and Margo safe was to stay away from them.

One day I got a letter from Margo. They had sent it to a P.O. Box under an alias.

Dearest Daniel:

I am writing to tell you that we have been well.
We have settled in a small house at the edge of
town. It has all the comforts of life but without
any connection to the outside world. We have no
internet, no TV. We turned off our cellphones.
We've taken precautions, just as you advised us.
But we don't need these things anyway; we have
books and each other. And Elliot has his math.
Once a week, a delivery man brings our groceries.

It is beautiful here. The house is near the base of the mountain, and each day its red surface shines with the rising sun. Throughout the day, its color changes with the changing sky. Every morning, Elliot takes his notebook and a little snack and goes there. He sits under the shade of the mountain and works on his math until lunch. Then we have lunch together. Sometimes in the afternoon, we hike to the top and stay until sunset. From here we can see the entire desert.

We've been more than well; we've been in heaven. It is paradise. We talk to each other. Elliot has never talked to me like this before. We talk about the future. A lot of times, we talk about you. You're more than a good friend to us; you're family. Please come and visit us soon.

Love,

M.

At last, I decided to visit Elliot and Margo. After all, it was my mission to protect Elliot and to goad him back to math. Their house was in Sedona, Arizona, at the edge of town, and so I took a bus to Phoenix, where I did my best to disappear from the satellites. Then I bought an old motorcycle to get to Sedona. I rode at a leisurely pace and took several detours and back roads. By late afternoon, I reached the house. It was even more beautiful than I had envisioned. The adobe house with a red door sat back away from the small road and could easily be missed. A wooden fence ran around the house, and the yard was rank with cacti.

"Elliot! Margo!" I called out from the gate. I headed hesitantly toward the house, not knowing for sure that it was the right one.

The door swung open, and Margo ran out.

"Oh, Daniel," she said.

Something was not right with her. Her eyes were brimming with tears. She was holding a cellphone.

"What's wrong?" I said.

"He's gone."

"What?"

"He went to his usual place this morning. He didn't come home for lunch, so I went out there to look for him. His shoes, his blanket, his notebooks, his snacks. Everything is there except for him," she said breathlessly.

"Show me where."

She led around the house to the back. Beyond the fence, a path led to the foot of the mountain. By a large boulder with a hollow base there was a Navajo blanket laid on the ground with Elliot's notebooks, walking shoes, his glasses, a bag of mixed nuts, and a bottle of water. When I saw the spot, I knew right away; I felt it in my gut, as if Elliot was telling me himself. He had escaped the simulation. Still, I had to check; I looked around. There was no sign of struggle, no other footprints except ours. I scanned the horizon, but there was nothing.

Margo cried.

"I was about to call you," she said, holding her cellphone.

"Did he say something this morning?"

"He has been going on about things being fake. That none of this was real. He said he found a way out."

"I'm sorry, but he's gone. Nobody took him. He left."

She cried, and I couldn't help but hug her.

"What do you mean he left?"

"He left this world. He found a way out. But I promise you'll see him again. One day."

"How can you promise something like that?"

When the time came for me to return to the real world, I would let Margo go in my place. She belonged out there with Elliot. Whether it was the end of the universe or the end of me, it made no difference to me. And now that Elliot had escaped to the real world, the world would soon end as it should. Everything would be reshuffled and restarted again. Nothing would be missed.

We sat down on the blanket. It was a great spot to sit. From here I could see the vast desert below. Behind me was the red surface of the mountain. It was magical. It didn't matter that none of this was real, that we were just two beings in a simulation. That she was with me was all that mattered. As the sun gleamed beautifully against the landscape, I held her hand and began to tell her the truth.

EPILOGUE

I have a confession to make.

It has been six months since Elliot left, and I have been living with Margo in the same house in Sedona. Things have been peaceful. Amid this tranquility, I've begun to learn the truth about myself. Each night, Margo and I would go to bed together, and each morning we would rise together. Full of memories of lust and passion and unrequited love, I would make love to her. Each time was as wonderful as compared to what I used to imagine it would be like to make love to her, when I didn't have her and could only dream. Each time, it was as if I felt love for the first time. There was something new about my feelings for her, each nuanced sensation filled excitement and discovery. During each physical interaction, it was as if I were making love to her for the first time; though

I have been with many women before, the physical acts were in themselves a discovery.

It was not only the lovemaking, but all the activities of life itself—waking up, brushing my teeth, shaving, taking a shower, making coffee, eating, smelling, and even relieving myself—seemed to take on a gap and were possible only following an act of remembering first. I found each act delightful. What's more, I've been seeing the earth as it is, without the flows of energy, without the silhouettes of ghosts. And I know for sure now that I lost my psychic ability when God put me back.

Then a couple of months ago, I began to notice the slightest awkwardness on Margo's part whenever we were close. At first, I attributed this to her missing Elliot and to her eventual reunion with him, because, if Elliot is out there waiting for her, she has been in fact cheating with me. When I tried to probe her feelings, she said that it might have been a mistake for us to be together. She said that she had thought she loved me as she did Elliot, but now she knew that we could only be friends.

This news came as a shock to me, but it forced me to face the truth. I have been sensing it in the back of my mind, and at last, I faced it squarely. After mulling about it for days, I've come to a conclusion. I must make a confession.

I am not Daniel.

It was I who killed Daniel. During our fight, we were equally matched. Remember how I said that at times it was as if our minds were linked, that I could feel his pain and he mine? When God made me, I was a perfect duplicate of Daniel, with one key difference. I had been given his memory, but he had lived his. He had lived countless iterations on this Earth, each time as a different life form; after each iteration his form had been dissected and reshuffled, but always retained something. He had in him thousands of years of sorrow, sadness, pain, and unfathomable injustice, but also joy, happiness, hope, and love. His sense of justice was all powerful, and so when we were at a deadly stalemate, his sense of fair play could not permit him to do what I did. After all his years on Earth, I would say that he has a soul.

Unencumbered by justice, I did what I needed to do to win. Biting his nose off was an act befitting a coward. I will forever be sorry and will bear that shame.

I am sure now that God knew exactly what he did. He gave me all of Daniel's memory the moment Daniel hit me. And then my mind was overwhelmed by pain, by an instinct to survive, and so after I killed Daniel, all I could remember was wanting to fight, to kill him. Afterward I became him. That's why I don't have any of Daniel's psychic abilities; these abilities have been born of this earth, this world; Daniel's mind and this world are linked through the countless iterations of simulation. That's why I find life new, each physical act a discovery. And that's why Margo cannot love me; her essence and Daniel's have been mixed and partitioned through the ages, just as theirs and Elliot's have. That's why her mind senses that I am not Daniel, her Daniel, her love.

Daniel is out there with Elliot. There was only one thing for me to do.

One morning, I took Margo to the same spot where Elliot had disappeared.

"What are we doing here?" Margo asked.

"It's time you go to Elliot," I said.

I wrote Elliot's equation, the correct one, in the air, and a needle's eye of blackness appeared. Sunlight began to swirl round and round and entered the black dot.

"All you have to do is to put your finger into the dot. You will go to Elliot," I said.

She looked at me with disbelief.

"Trust me," I said. "Say hi to Elliot for me. And Daniel too."

"Daniel?"

"Yes, the real Daniel. Tell him I'm sorry."

She gave me a kiss, and then she was gone.

As for me, I will stay and wander the earth. Until I return to the real world, I will become part of this world and relive a different life form through each simulation.

I hope I will eventually take on all forms of the animals and the plants, and experience all the sensations and sentiments of this world. Perhaps one day, I, like Daniel, will have something which even God cannot take away: a soul.

THE END.